34 PIECES OF YOU

CARMEN RODRIGUES

SIMON PULSE
NEW YORK LONDON TORONTO SYDNEY NEW DELHI

SIMON PULSE
An imprint of Simon & Schuster Children's Publishing Division
1230 Avenue of the Americas, New York, NY 10020
First Simon Pulse hardcover edition September 2012
Copyright © 2012 by Carmen Rodrigues
All rights reserved, including the right of reproduction in whole or in part in any form.
SIMON PULSE and colophon are registered trademarks of Simon & Schuster, Inc.
For information about special discounts for bulk purchases, please contact
Simon & Schuster Special Sales at 1-866-506-1949
or business@simonandschuster.com.
The Simon & Schuster Speakers Bureau can bring authors to your live event.
For more information or to book an event contact the Simon & Schuster Speakers
Bureau at 1-866-248-3049 or visit our website at www.simonspeakers.com.
Designed by Mike Rosamilia
The text of this book was set in Adobe Garamond Pro.
Manufactured in the United States of America
2 4 6 8 10 9 7 5 3
Library of Congress Cataloging-in-Publication Data
Rodrigues, Carmen.
34 pieces of you / by Carmen Rodrigues.
p. cm.
Summary: When Ellie dies of a drug overdose, her brother, her best
friend, and her best friend's sister face painful secrets of their own
when they try to uncover the truth about Ellie's death.
ISBN 978-1-4424-3906-1 (alk. paper)
[1. Death—Fiction. 2. Secrets—Fiction.] I. Title.
II. Title: Thirty-four pieces of you.
PZ7.R61875Aam 2012
[Fic]—dc23
2011045279
ISBN 978-1-4424-3908-5 (eBook)

To Snowy,
proof that prayers are answered,
and that faith,
above all else,
will lead you home

Acknowledgments

—Tremendous gratitude to my editor, Jen Klonsky, for her sharp eyes, accurate red pen, and humanizing sense of humor. I am so thrilled to have worked with you on this project and look forward to many more in our future.

—Big thanks to the lovely behind-the-scenes people at Simon & Schuster: Mara Anastas, Laura Antonacci, Bethany Buck, Paul Crichton, Katherine Devendorf, Michelle Fadlalla, Russell Gordon, Jessica Handelman, Lucille Rettino, Dawn Ryan, Sara Saidlower, Michael Strother, Carolyn Swerdloff, Venessa Williams—and the wonderful sales force, who ensure that this novel finds readers.

—Much appreciation to my fantastic agent, Steven Chudney, for believing in this project and me.

—Special love to Random House (Germany) for giving this novel a second home and second language.

—Big thanks to my peers and professors in the creative writing department at the University of North Carolina Wilmington for your faith, feedback, and guidance. Additionally, I owe a special gratitude to my thesis readers: Wendy Brenner, Clyde Edgerton, and Robert Siegel. The education I received at UNCW was top-notch.

I'm so glad to have once been a part of your intoxicatingly creative world.

—Gratitude to my favorite fellows, the D.O.T.B. crew: Nathan Johnson, Trey Morehouse, and Eric Tran. Your home was often my home, and for that I am grateful.

—Buckets of love with whipped cream and sprinkles on top to my friends/confidants/second family: Amy Risher, Lindsay Key, Kiki Vera Johnson, Alison Harney, Brian McCann, Kate Rogers, and Peter Trachtenberg. You graciously listened to my endless worries, schemes, and plans for multiple revisions, and despite your exhaustion, continued to provide encouragement and love. God bless you.

—Thanks to my writing buddies. In particular, Bethany Griffin, who said from the very beginning, "I love it!" Those kind words kept me going. To Melissa Walker and Nina de Gramont, for your willingness to always give me advice. And to Matt de la Peña, who popped up out of the blue and continues to believe in me.

—To those whom I may have forgotten, I give you my thanks and ask for your forgiveness.

—To my dear family: Mom, I love you more than the stars. Thank you for instilling such a faith in God in me. Natalie, thank you for your stories. Your unique imagination sparked mine. Walter, you're the best bro a girl can have. You constantly surprise me with how wonderful you are. And to Suzette, my twin in spirit and blood, may the years be long and the road traveled soft. And to the rest of my family: There is a place in my heart I keep warm and safe for you.

—And, most important, thank you to God, my guiding light above, for all that I am and all that I continue to be.

Jessie
NOVEMBER.

That Saturday I woke before dawn to the sounds of sirens, the doorbell ringing, and Mattie crying. I sat up, glanced at Sarah's empty bed, and then the door creaked open. Meg stood there in her polka-dotted pj's and fuzzy slippers, framed by the light from the hallway.

"What's going on?" I murmured.

"I don't know. They won't tell me." She flipped on the light.

"God, Meg!" I shielded my eyes. "Turn it off."

"Sorry." She flicked the switch and the room went dark.

"Is it Old Mrs. Sawyer again?"

"I don't know."

I grabbed the robe hanging off my bedpost and wrapped it around me. The house was chilly, and the cold only added to my exhaustion. I thought about going back to bed, but Meg was still there, staring at me expectantly. Below, our parents' voices grew louder. A door slammed, and the sirens started up again. I peeked out the window just as the ambulance rushed away.

The street was bright with porch lights. A few neighbors huddled together in front of Mr. Lumpnick's yard, talking. I scanned the group, looking for Sarah and her best friend, Ellie, but wasn't surprised when I didn't find them. Just because I had spent last night moping didn't mean they hadn't spent it partying. They were probably passed out somewhere.

Meg peered over my shoulder. "Mom said to come get you."

I followed Meg down the stairs and thought about the possibilities for that ambulance. Since most of our other neighbors were standing in Mr. Lumpnick's yard, I decided it had probably come for Old Mrs. Sawyer.

Mattie was wrapped in a blanket on the living-room sofa, sucking her thumb as she watched her *Dora the Explorer* DVD. Mom stood a short distance away, in the kitchen, her back visible from the hall. She was talking on the phone. I gave Meg a reassuring smile and said, "It's okay. See how calm Mom sounds?"

CARMEN RODRIGUES

Meg leaned forward to grasp her tone, which was steady enough for such an unexpected morning. "Go on." I nudged her toward the living room and watched as she curled into the couch, covering her lower legs with part of Mattie's blanket.

In the kitchen, Mom stood quietly beside the phone, her hand still holding the receiver to the base. There was something about her stance that made my numbness fade. "Everything okay?" I asked.

She turned to me, her skin blotchy from crying.

"Mom?"

"Jess." She came to me, grabbed my shoulders, and pulled me close. She whispered in my ear, "Sarah's been in an accident, and I have to go meet your dad at the hospital. Okay? But it's going to be fine. I just don't want to upset your sisters. So let's talk quietly for now."

She stepped back and took my hands. She searched my eyes, offering me a shaky smile, but I saw the tears waiting.

A lump formed in my throat. I imagined Sarah in the role of Old Mrs. Sawyer, slipping in the shower, breaking her collarbone or something, the ambulance rushing her and Dad to the hospital while Mom sat in the kitchen, writing speeches about the perils of underage drinking. And there was little doubt in my mind that my sister and Ellie had been drinking.

"Is she really going to be okay?" I asked, because parents had a way of lying to you so you wouldn't freak out. I wanted to know the truth. "Seriously, Mom."

Mom nodded, dropping my hands to push the hair from her face. "We think so. She was still coherent when Tommy found her . . . found . . ." She put a hand to her mouth and looked out the kitchen window that faced Ellie's house. I followed her gaze. The lights were on there, but the driveway was empty.

"Tommy was there?" Tommy was another kid from the neighborhood. The scenario changed again to include him: Sarah still in the shower, drunk, but now Tommy with Ellie, his hands crawling over her body. "What did Ellie say, exactly?" My voice turned sharp, the suspicion so strong it made my skin tingle. "Is she at home? Can I talk to her real quick before you go?" I wanted answers that I knew only Ellie could give, and I wanted to tell her she was an awful person for misleading me and betraying Sarah. I wanted to tell her that we would never forgive her.

Mom was at the window now.

"Mom?"

She sank onto her knees and buried her head in her hands.

"Mom?"

"Tommy found them, but he wasn't there. The accident,

Jess . . . it was Ellie, too . . ." She turned to me, tears streaming down her face.

And again the scenarios shifted until finally I understood. I gripped the edge of the table, willing the room to stop spinning, my breath to return.

"It's not good, Jess," she said. "Ellie . . . it's not good."

The heat clicked on, and a warm burst of air flowed across my calves. The room spun quickly now, flashes of colors that disappeared when I closed my eyes. Every noise in the world was silenced.

Then a small, cold hand slipped into mine. A soft voice whispered my name. I opened my eyes. Mattie stood beside me, her eyes curious but absent of fear.

1.

You said, "Ellie, this is the truth,
everybody leaves. <u>Everybody</u>."
I was just seven, and when I
reached for you, you were where
death and absence and missing
take you. You were where bad
husbands disappear to. And you
were whispering, "Just ask them."

Sarah

AFTER. NOVEMBER.

Concerned Therapist taps her pencil on her notepad and smiles. This is not because today is a pleasant day, and the birds outside Smith Memorial Hospital are chirping, and the sun has created rainbow patterns on the worn linoleum floor. No, it's because it's one of her settings. She has three: Concerned. Reassuring. Empathetic.

"Sarah," she prompts again. "Do you recall saying that in our last conversation?"

I tug down the sleeves of my flannel pajamas, wondering why the junior psych ward is so cold, and say in a weary voice, "Really, I'm sorry. I don't."

Concerned Therapist consults her folder, flips back a few

pages on her clipboard. She says that the last time she came to visit, I remembered some things. She changes gears from Reassuring setting to Concerned setting, her thick eyebrows forming a rolling caterpillar above dime-size brown eyes. When I don't budge—not because I don't want to but because I honestly don't remember what I said the last time—she leans forward, one elbow pressed into the soft chocolate-colored skin above her knee. Her full lips turn downward into Empathetic setting.

"Sarah, I know this is hard for you, but can you try? Ellie was your best friend. I'm sure you're incredibly confused right now. Can we talk about that a little?"

This is not a subject I want to talk about, but it *is* a subject I *have* to talk about. Tomorrow I'll be released from the hospital, and before they discharge me, I have to perform this song and dance. "It's sad, and I'm really upset about it," I say finally.

Concerned Therapist motions for me to continue. Because it's true, I say, "It was an accident, a stupid accident." Then I stop talking, because here it is again, the bubble in my chest. The last time I felt it was when I overheard the doctors tell my parents, "You're lucky she's alive. An overdose like this . . . Well, she's lucky things didn't turn out for her the way they did for her friend."

This isn't true—this whole overdose business. At least not the way the doctors make it sound. I tried to explain this to one of my doctors, but all he did was nod politely, like he didn't believe me. And that made me hold on to this truth: I don't have to explain anything to anyone. I just have to tell them enough to be released.

Stoic. That's the word I keep putting in my mind. I hold it there like a ball suspended in midair. It takes a lot of energy to keep a ball in midair when you're not using your hands. When you're just using your mind, it's a miracle if you can get the ball off the ground.

And so that's what I do: I use all my energy to stoically stare at this woman's pinched face, but after a while it doesn't seem so pinched. That's because she continues to speak to me in that encouraging way of hers. And her face starts to seem kind and generous. And my heart breaks open a little and comes into contact with the thoughts that pop into my head: *How can Ellie be dead? And where does that minute go, that minute that separates life from death? I want those sixty seconds back.*

Concerned Therapist studies me. "Tell me about the accident, Sarah."

"We did this before," I remind her, and luckily her pinched face returns.

"But tell me again," she says.

"Because . . ." The word fades, like I don't have the strength to make it whole, and I hate myself for sounding weak in front of her.

"Because?" Concerned Therapist says. Her bony shoulders curve forward. Her hand flickers at her side. I wonder if she wants to reach out to me. "Sarah, this is a safe place. You can say anything."

This is the big lie adults tell you: that you can say anything. But the minute you say anything about anything, you're given this lecture about how you can make your life better and what you should do but aren't doing. And you're told how *you* screwed it up and what *they're* going to do to make it better. And how this will be the absolute last time they help you, and isn't it time you grew up already?

I could even hear my mom's voice whispering in my ear: *It's simple, Sarah. A + B + C = Problem solved.*

So I don't say anything. Instead I close my eyes, and even though I don't want it, Ellie is there. And it's five days before, and she's twirling and laughing and holding the pills. And she's calling out to me. She's saying, *Catch up, Sarah. Catch up.*

"Sarah?" Concerned Therapist places her hand lightly on my

arm. Goose bumps spread across my flesh. "Are you okay?" she asks, but I hold still.

I hold still, and when I am composed, I say, "It was an accident. I'm sorry about Ellie, but we never meant for any of this to happen. We were just being stupid. We just—"

It is here that I put my hand to my mouth. The therapist hands me a tissue and nods her approval. The bubble in my chest expands but does not burst. It holds steady. Waiting.

There is one solid truth in my life: When visiting hours are over, Glenn will still come to see me.

Glenn isn't my biological dad—no, that man abandoned me before I was born—but he's my *real dad* and so I call him Dad, because he's always been there for me. When I look at him, I see all these pictures. Pictures of him in his marines uniform the day he married my mom, my life still forming in her swollen belly. Pictures of him at my third birthday party, our hands covered in sticky white icing. Pictures of him at the births of my younger sisters, his real daughters—first Jessie, then Meg, then Mattie. Even now, I snap a picture of this moment to place in my internal box of proof that Glenn loves me.

My dad is a handsome man with large eyes and limbs as solid as tree trunks. He understands that I haven't looked at anyone in days. He says, "I should have been here. I should've known."

"She can come home tomorrow, Glenn." That's my mom speaking. She's not at all like my dad. She's small, with blond hair, pale skin, and nervous hands. Mom hates her nervous hands. For a second she stands beside my dad, her hands buried deep in her pockets. But before long she's tidying up the space and making small talk. She says things like, "How are you today? Did you sleep well? Do you need something? Look at that tree outside. Isn't it lovely? Tommy asked after you. Isn't that nice? Do you need more pillows? I can ask the nurse for more pillows. Why is it impossibly cold in here?"

"Sarah." Here is my dad, again. His smile is cautious. "You can come home tomorrow. That's good, isn't it?"

And here's where I nod. I do this so they can see I'm responsive. "Responsive" is a big word in the junior psych ward. If I stop acting responsive, I might never get out. So I'm careful to respond and to hide that I've been crying a lot. But when I speak, my throat is parched. "I want to go to Ellie's funeral so I can say good-bye." These are difficult words to string together. Especially the part about my best friend's funeral. Especially the part about good-bye.

There is a silence that's not silent at all. It's exchanged

glances and shuffling hands. My father clears his throat. "Sarah," he says. "Sarah, that's not going to be possible—"

And my mom gently touches the side of my face and says, "Honey . . ." But the word is soft, more like a prayer.

Then Dad says, "Sarah . . ."

And I say, "I'm here." Because I think that's what they need me to say, but now my dad is looking beyond me. He's looking outside the room to the beech tree visible from my hospital window. I look too. The branches are like a thousand arms pleading with the sky. When I look back, my dad is watching me. He swipes a quick hand beneath his eyes. Then he calls to my mom like he doesn't know what to say. He says, "Serena . . ."

"Glenn . . ." Mom places her hand on my dad's neck. He is the person she understands best, not the rest of us, who came from her body. I think we're a mystery to her. "Just tell her."

And this is where he looks at me. He rests his palm on the back of my head. His hand encompasses my entire scalp, and there is safety in this knowledge that he can still fit parts of me beneath the callused strength of his fingertips. He says, "Ellie was cremated. They're spreading her ashes today before her mother leaves on some kind of retreat."

And then there is silence and gasping. Minutes later, I realize I am the one gasping. I make myself stop. I tell them I am sorry.

"It's okay" is what my dad says.

"You'll get better. Give it time," is what my mom says.

We are silent for a long while. We are silent until we are a calm, picture-perfect family: a good mommy, a good daddy, a good daughter. And in the silence I suddenly understand the many ways a person can die but still be alive.

2.

That year Dad left us, I
pressed my ear to the wall
between our bedrooms,
listening to your quiet cries.

Jake

AFTER. NOVEMBER.

Mom says, "There's no way you could have known." After I came home from NYU, after I accompanied her to the morgue, after she dug manicured nails into the center of my palm, after the funeral arrangements were made, after the viewing of my sister's body, Mom finally looks at me and says, "Jake . . ." Then she taps her foot nervously against the bottom of the sofa and looks away.

Her eyes are bloodshot, but she is uncharacteristically sober, and because of this and her grief, her hands shake cigarette ash everywhere, coating the beige carpet with a thin layer of gray. She says, "There's no way you could have known." Then she lays a cold compress against her skin.

I look away, toward Ellie's room. The door is locked, as if my mother wants to lock away the memory of that night when Tommy found Ellie's body cold and motionless on the bedroom floor. One part of me is relieved the room is inaccessible, but another part wants to break that door down and bury myself in the pieces of her abandoned life.

Mom scoots closer on the sofa, presses her wet hand over mine. I try, like always, not to cringe. I don't confess, *I knew something was wrong.* I don't confess, *It was my fault.* Instead I watch her eyes search the room for an anchor, something to weigh her down, and I think about the slight tremor that takes her voice and spins it like a Ferris wheel.

"I want to scream," Mom says quietly, but I know she won't. She doesn't know how. She's a doctor, a mother, and an alcoholic, but, surprisingly, none of these pursuits ever prompt her to raise her voice, not at me or my sister or any of her three idiot husbands. My mother turns things inward, so that her insides must be as black and murky as a landfill.

She clears her throat. "Your father will be here for the service tomorrow. We'll bury Ellie's ashes underneath a tree, beside that creek she loved when she was little." Her voice reduces then, suddenly the density of decomposing leaves. She struggles for breath, but I do not turn my head. "Do you remember Falling Creek?"

CARMEN RODRIGUES

I cover her hand with mine and say, "It's a good spot, Mom. A real good spot." She starts to cry then. Her shoulder slumps against mine; her tears hit the collar of my shirt. A low moan emerges from her lips. I wait for it to grow, to swirl around the room until it settles across our shoulders like a shroud. But the whimper stays low, the frequency of a turned-down radio. Eventually it stops, but not the crying. The crying remains.

BEFORE. JUNE.

The thick black smoke from the U-Haul's exhaust pipe burned the sides of my legs, and Ellie stood, swinging her willowy arms, scratching her nose. I was leaving her to go to college, and she was edgy, her cigarette nearly gone. She tossed it to the ground, stomped it out with the tip of her flip-flop, and said, "Can't you go to community college here or something? Why do you have to go so far? Why NYU?"

"Ellie, please."

"I just don't understand why you have to leave so early. Why can't you leave in August like everyone else?"

"Because," I said. "I have to take those summer classes. You know they told me I have to." She was silent because she knew all of this to be true. That a nearly perfect SAT score and solid essay earned me my spot at NYU, but Admissions, worried about my spotty GPA, insisted I take summer classes to "improve my chances of succeeding at the collegiate level." What she didn't know was how grateful I was to leave early.

Our uncle was in the U-Haul, impatiently waiting. I glanced at him, took in his newly shaved head, the bright white of his eyes, and remembered how only years before, after the holidays I would find him slumped over the kitchen table, still too drunk to drive, his hand clutching the carcass of a cigarette.

My uncle was an asshole when he drank, and during those moments of his incapacitation, I'd take my revenge. Prop my feet dangerously close to the curl of his lip. Set the sole of my shoe against that slip of pink flesh. Still he slept. So I'd slide a hand into his back pocket, steal whatever I could find. Then I'd ride my bike to the bookstore. Buy a graphic novel or a CD. And when I returned, he'd still be there, his hand still clutching.

Now he was sober. Had been ever since he met his second wife, Matilda. And he was blowing the horn again and giving me a look that said, *Come on already*. And then he leaned out the window and yelled, "Jake, hurry up already!"

"You know I have to go." I looked past Ellie's sad eyes to Sarah and Tommy, who stood just a short distance away, holding hands. And even farther away, behind them, stood my mom with her husband, the latest—and, hopefully, last—asshole.

I don't know why, because you would think seeing Tommy with Sarah or seeing my mom with the jerk would make me want to leave, but in that moment I realized leaving was harder than I imagined. Still, there was a part of me that just wanted out and away from all of this confusion. From my on-and-off-again situation with Sarah. From those moments between us that seemed real but dissolved in memory. From the drama of Ellie, her moodiness and urges to self-destruct. From the weirdness that had started with Tommy ever since he and Sarah began hooking up last year.

"Ellie, I've got to get out of here." I touched her arm, wrapped my hand around her wrist and swung it back and forth, like when we were kids and touching each other wasn't so awkward.

Behind her, Tommy said, "Jake, your uncle, man. He's, like, hitting the steering wheel and shit." I glanced at my uncle. He was hitting the steering wheel with his balled-up fist.

"Jake?" Mom stepped forward. The rings around her eyes hovered like dark clouds, proof she'd always be one step away from a hangover. Sarah stepped forward too. And when our eyes met, I was reminded of the night before, when she'd come to me, said she wanted to talk, her hands buried in the pockets of her cutoff jeans. How the shape of her lean thighs beneath the denim made me want to touch her, but I didn't, not even when she placed a confident hand in the space between my shoulder blades.

Sarah was like a roller coaster. Just when I thought the ride was over, she'd peak again, another hill rising against a dimming blue sky. Each time, the hill would be bigger and scarier than the last. Still, there were days when I wanted her fingers running lightly over my forearm or her hand rubbing that tender spot between my shoulders. And I'd recall with clarity the feeling of her palm against the back of my neck. The way she would gently press in circular motions until my head fell forward and I felt—just for that moment—a complete sense of surrender.

Maybe that was why the night before, when she'd placed her hands on me, I'd let myself take in the first waves of her touch. But as her voice grew more confident, as her belief in the possibility of us solidified, I'd moved beyond her reach. The truth was, I didn't trust her. How could I? Even right now, after everything that had happened between us in the last five years, she stood there, holding my best friend's hand.

Ellie kicked me lightly, and I looked back at her. The soft spots beneath her eyes were blue from lack of sleep. She pulled her wrist away and said, "Tell me you didn't, Jake. You promised you wouldn't."

"Do what?" I said, but I knew she was talking about Sarah.

She never wanted me near her. Never wanted me to *fuck it up*. Because that's the other truth: I wasn't exactly nice to girls.

"Come on, Jake." She looked down at the grass, so that her long blond hair fell across her face. I could tell she was crying. I couldn't remember the last time I had seen her cry. But if I had to pinpoint an exact period, I'd say it was the summer she was eleven and she came to me, hands trembling between my palms, and told me what Evan, our first step-asshole, had done to her.

"Come on, Ellie." I stepped closer but didn't touch her like before. "Don't."

She laughed and wiped her eyes with the underside of her tank top, leaving streaks of black mascara on the thin fabric. She said, "God!" Then louder, "God! Look at this. I'm such a fucking baby." Her tears came down a little harder.

I pulled her closer and held her until she stopped squirming. The side of my neck grew wet from her crying.

She whispered, "If I need you, you'll come back for me?"

"Yes, of course." I pulled her in as close as I could, and wondered if she understood how much I had watched out for her these last ten years, since our father left. How sometimes I still had nightmares about Evan's hands touching her, hurting her.

She said, "You promise me. If I need you, you'll come back to me."

"Always, Ellie. Always."

Behind us, Sarah watched. And when our eyes locked, I felt that pain I got whenever she was around. That pain of knowing that sometimes the things I want aren't the things I need, but not knowing, exactly, how to let those things go.

My uncle honked the horn and revved the engine. Ellie took a step back. She said, "You better go." Then she looked away from me and pushed another cigarette between her lips. I lit it for her, watching as she tucked her hair behind her ears. Some strands still clung to her damp face. She didn't look at me, but she said, "I love you, Jake."

I looked at the ground. I said, "I know, Ellie. I know."

3.

This house is lonely.
    I want . . .

Jessie

AFTER. JANUARY.

After Sarah came home from the hospital, Mom moved her from our shared bedroom into the guest room on the first floor. Now I spend a lot of time alone, thinking. I think a lot about Sarah, a lot about Ellie, a lot about me, who I am, and who I'm meant to be.

My mom thinks that we—her daughters—all have types. Sarah is the reactive type. Meg is the silly type. Mattie is the sweet and cuddly type. I'm the thoughtful type. Or at least that's what Mom always says: *Jess, you're just so thoughtful! How did I end up with such a thoughtful daughter?*

Still, before Ellie died, I liked to do other things besides think. I liked to hang out in front of my house or go to the movies or run around crazy with my best friend, Lola. Before Ellie died, I liked to pretend that I was someone else, someone who wasn't so . . . thoughtful. But now it seems like there's no use in pretending.

I think when someone you know dies, something inside of you changes—like some supernatural creature came into your room and took his big, supernatural hands and rearranged your entire DNA.

I tried to explain this to Lola once, but she just looked at me like I was crazy. Then she asked me why I was suddenly so waiflike, like a shorter version of Kate Moss. She actually took out a pen, asked me to describe my diet *secrets*, and said that no matter how many miles she ran, her curvaceous hips wouldn't shrink fast enough to fit into the size 2 jeans she imagines herself wearing.

I waited a few minutes to answer. Then I told her the truth: "My diet's simple, so simple you don't even have to write it down. Just throw up after most meals, and sometimes don't eat at all."

I had never said this out loud, so I gave us both time to process the seriousness of my words, but she just thumped me on the head with her fuzzy blue pen and said, "That's brilliant!" And, after that, she never mentioned it again. Although I noticed she lost five pounds in the next month.

In total, I've lost fifteen pounds, but except for Lola, nobody's asking why. I suppose that's because Mom's too busy worrying about Sarah, Dad's too busy worrying about Mom, and Meg and Mattie are too busy worrying about themselves to notice my incredible disappearing act.

Besides, it's not a big deal. I'm okay. I don't have a problem. I definitely don't have an eating disorder. I don't think I look fat. I don't want to be this skinny. I don't think I look good this skinny, but I can't help it. I can't change it.

When I eat food—that is, if I feel like eating at all—it won't stay down. There's just not enough room. I guess that's what happens when your belly is filled with secrets.

Ever since Sarah came home from the hospital, there's been a lot of tiptoeing. We tiptoe around conversations in the dining room when we all sit down to family dinners. We tiptoe through the hallway, in case Sarah might hear our footsteps clunking past the guest-bedroom door. Even now I tread as softly as I can. Lola follows, laughing.

"Why are you walking so slow?" She bumps me from behind, and I fall into a table with the slightest thud. The noise shocks me. I have this irrational thought of shoving her face into the wall, but I push that feeling away—mark it as another typical Lola thing not worth thinking about.

When we hit the second-floor landing, I pause to take a deep breath.

"Jesus," Lola says, "are we going to stand here forever?" She nudges my shoulder until I start walking again. I think of something sharp to say, but when I open my mouth, I only explain. "I told you. We have to be quiet downstairs because of Sarah."

Lola says, "I don't understand why you have to be quiet for her at all." Then she dives onto my bed and tosses all my stuffed animals—the ones she wants me to throw away because fifteen-year-olds shouldn't have toys—onto the floor. My favorite, Mr. Big Butt Bear, stares at me accusingly.

Before, I might have yelled at Lola, but now I only pick up Mr. Big Butt Bear and sit with him on the carpet, my back against the bedroom door. Downstairs another door creaks open, and I realize we've woken Sarah. The guilt sets in immediately. It's a trait I inherited from my father. Sarah says you can get him to do anything if you make him feel guilty enough.

Below are scratching noises, like Sarah's dragging a chair back and forth. It's weird, because the more I listen to the sounds and start to identify them, the more I can picture what's going on.

In the movie in my head, Sarah drags a dining-room chair through the living room and places it underneath the archway that leads into Dad's den. She stands on the chair, reaching her hand up to feel along the decorative molding. She searches for the key to the liquor cabinet but doesn't find it there. After the hospital, Dad moved the key. I saw him do it.

Now she drags the chair back into the dining room. She paces the living room. She lifts up porcelain figurines, wooden picture frames, maybe even Mattie's plastic toys, and searches for the hidden key. She goes into the den and rifles through Dad's desk, but she's very careful not to disturb his things. She doesn't want to get caught. Still, she searches thoroughly, but she doesn't find the key, because it's not there.

Now she's near Dad's desk, probably leaning back against it. Her mind races: *Where is it? Where is it? Where is it?* And her veins chime in: *Need it. Need it. Need it.* She glances at the clock on the wall. She takes the steps, one at a time. She pauses outside the room and debates knocking. She turns the doorknob and pushes hard because I'm blocking the door.

And there she is, looking down at me through this narrow crack. She doesn't acknowledge Lola. She doesn't see Mr. Big Butt Bear. She doesn't even see me, really. But she stares at me, and her stare is panicked.

"Where is it?" she asks.

"Where's what?"

"You know what." She nudges the door some more, and I slide over a few inches.

"I don't know what you're talking about," I say.

Lola is quiet. I think Sarah scares her. It's easy to scare people once they've heard a rumor that you've killed your best friend. If I killed Lola, I wouldn't have to hear her stupid stories and put up with her bossy commands. She'd be dead. She'd be silent. The thought makes me feel horrible, yet it is there.

Sarah continues to stare. She nudges the door again. I'm sure there's going to be a big bruise on my leg in the morning. She says, "Don't do this," in a voice that doesn't really belong to her— the real Sarah hasn't spoken to me since Ellie died. Still, I hear this Sarah's voice clearly, and I know what she's really saying is, *Please don't make me beg, not in front of Lola.*

It's hard for me. I'm not supposed to have the answer to this question. I'm not supposed to even know what she's talking about. But we both know I do. We both know that's the problem with me. I see everything.

"It's taped underneath the rug in Dad's office." My voice is meek, because I know I'm betraying Dad. I'm betraying Mom. I'm betraying me. And worst of all, I'm betraying Sarah.

Sarah shuts the door, and I stare at it real hard. From behind me Lola goes, "Fuck. What's her problem?"

"Nothing."

"Nothing?" Lola says, like that's the stupidest thing I've ever said.

"Yeah, nothing," I say, because it's true. The fact is, when Ellie died, the things that used to matter stopped mattering. And now all of this, absolutely all of this, means nothing at all.

4.

Do you remember when you were eleven and you saved that mouse from a trap set by your father? How you walked a mile into the woods to find a safe place to set it free.

Sarah
AFTER. JANUARY.

At home, my sisters stare at me like I'm some sort of alien or something, like they've never seen someone who doesn't want to leave the house, who lets days slide by like raindrops down a windowpane. "Sarah?" Chubby Mattie, with her first adult tooth partially grown in, is the bravest. She sits with me each day, watches me be lethargic. Only, she doesn't know what "lethargic" means, because they don't learn three-syllable words in kindergarten.

Mattie wears clothes that never match and says ridiculous things like, *Did you know that mermaids live in the ocean and not the pool? And when they poop, their poop floats around them because they don't have toilets in the ocean.*

Today, Mattie carries a Dora the Explorer book tenderly in

one hand. "Can we read?" she asks, and it's only because she smells like talcum powder, has chunky thighs, and doesn't ask serious questions that I don't hesitate to pull her onto my lap and bury my face in the sweetness of her hair.

Mattie loves to read. Was born to read. I love to listen to Mattie read. The way her voice rises two octaves above everyone else's. The way her words collide—an endless train of sounds that doesn't require breath.

But today when Mattie reads, I cannot listen, because Mom is yelling at Dad, their raised voices spilling out of their bedroom.

"We're not helping her" is what Mom says.

"Serena" is what Dad says. "Be patient, please. She'll come around. She needs space—"

"You're only home for a few days at a time. You don't know what it's like for her, for the girls to see her like this. You don't know what it's like for me. All she does is lie in bed and watch TV. She doesn't bother with her home-school assignments. Glenn, she won't graduate this year if—"

"Is that so important?"

Mom is quiet. I imagine she's trying to reel in her rising panic because Dad doesn't like scenes. But soon she's back on it. She says, "Look, she won't—"

"*Please*, I just got home. I haven't even showered."

And here I remember how tired he looked when he walked through the door, his work boots caked with mud. But Mom does not seem to recall this. She snaps, "Well, when? When will we talk about it? It's been months. We have to do something—" Her voice breaks mid-sentence, and now all I can hear is the much quieter sound of her crying.

Mattie tugs my hand to remind me of her existence. I pull her close, kiss the top of her head. She continues reading, but I do not listen.

"Dude." Tommy rocks back on a chair beside my bedroom window. It is my favorite place to sit and stare at the world outside. "You know you're in bad shape when your mom keeps asking me to come over."

Tommy is my friend, neighbor, former classmate. He's also a burnout, smoker, blunter, whatever. He's known me since before I was labeled difficult, required constant surveillance, and turned Mom's blond hair partially gray. "C'mon, girl in the moon, don't just sit there staring outside. Talk to me." Tommy smoked before he came over. I see it in his eyes.

"What do you want to talk about?" I ask with little interest. It's been one of those long days where nothing happens, so it seems even longer.

"I don't know, man. You want me to tell you about school?" Tommy laughs. "Wow. I sounded like I cared. You know"—he clears his throat seductively—"caring is sharing, unless you're sharing herpes."

"Fuck you, Tommy," I say, and think about Ellie and how she loved Tommy's fucked-up sayings.

Ellie would say in her very best Forrest Gump voice: *Life is like a box of chocolates: You never know what you're going to get.*

And Tommy would respond in a TV-announcer voice: *Mom, I'm worried. There's an intergalactic burn in Uranus.*

And then Ellie would do something ridiculous, like the pee-pee dance, and say in a very melodramatic, Shakespearean way: *To pee or not to pee, that is the question.*

And then Tommy would sing: *Oh, say can you pee, by the dawn's early light. What so proudly we sprayed at the twilight's last whizzing . . .*

And through it all they'd laugh—Tommy because he thought he was funny, and Ellie because she was making fun of him—and sometimes I felt like an outsider just watching them.

"Don't you miss her?" Despite how I feel on the inside, my voice is steady.

"Huh?" Tommy shakes his head, like he doesn't know who "her" is. His eyes narrow, and his gaze seems strictly focused on my toes.

Ever since I left school, ever since I stopped existing in the outside world, Tommy has visited every Sunday, but not once has he mentioned Ellie. "Ellie. Don't you miss her?"

"C'mon, *Sarah* . . ." Tommy's feet drop to the polished wood floor. He picks at a string that slowly unravels the hem of his shirt.

"I'm not trying to bring you down." My heart beats faster as I remember that night, the way those purple capsules rained down on us and how Ellie's voice followed: *Catch up, Sarah. Catch up.* I take a deep breath. "I just want to know if you miss her."

Tommy grabs me, pulls me close enough to hear his heart, so fragile beneath his skin. He kisses me, gently caresses my back, and says, "I miss her so much, you know." Then he says it again: "You know that." And I do know. And I feel bad for making him tell me, for putting this between us. And in my guilt, I wrap myself around him. I kiss him clean. I pray for his hands to transcend my disappearing skin to free what hides inside.

An hour later, we are on my bed—all tangled feet, messed-up sheets, and my head cradled on his chest. His hands trace the faint scars across my stomach—scars from a few years ago.

The first time I caught Ellie cutting herself, she stood in

the supply closet of our middle school's art room, pressing an X-ACTO knife to the pale flesh of her inner thigh.

"It's not a big deal," she said when she saw my surprise.

I stepped over the boxes of supplies and watched the blood trickle down her leg. "Why do it at all?"

We were fourteen, and every month we became a greater danger to ourselves and each other.

Ellie licked her index finger and used the tip to blend a streak of blood into her skin. "I don't know. You tell me." She held out the blade, still slick with her blood. "There's time," she said when I glanced anxiously at the door.

I didn't want there to be time. But I also didn't want there to *not* be time. Ellie had this way of pushing me past what felt logical into some other realm of what felt good because it was so wrong. Like together we'd escape to a place that had nothing to do with being good or in control. A place where we could make mistakes and know that at least they were our own.

I took the blade, feeling instantly light-headed, the room suddenly blurry around the edges. Slowly, I lifted my shirt, aware of her intense gaze, and found a spot below the lip of my panties.

"It'll be like we're blood sisters," Ellie said. She watched as I made that first incision, laughing softly when I gasped. My skin gave way to a trickle of blood that seeped into my cotton underwear. Slowly the room came back into focus, but my breathing remained erratic. Ellie smiled and said, "Forever sisters."

It was the biggest lie she ever told me.

Tommy burrows his chin into my messy hair, and I bring myself back to the present. "Your house is so quiet," he says. And it's true, the house is so quiet when my dad is away and my mom has taken my sisters out for an afternoon movie. That's what Mom does when Tommy comes over on Sundays. She clears the house, hoping, I bet, that Tommy will perform a magic trick in her absence. That I'll return to that other version of myself—that version that she didn't exactly like but that is still better than the one she has now.

Tommy wraps his arms around me, clears his throat nervously. "There's something I want to tell you about Ellie."

"Okay . . ." I look up at him, take in his anxious expression. I give him some time, but after a few minutes I ask, "Are you going to tell me or what?"

"Yeah, just give me a sec."

"What's the big deal? Go on."

"Um, well." He sighs. "Remember how you and I got into a fight a few days before . . ." He pauses. "You know, before . . . Ellie died?"

"Yeah." We were always going back and forth—never quite sure if we liked or hated each other—but our fight that night was the worst we'd had yet. And I was convinced we were finally done, but then everything happened with Ellie.

"Well, after that, Ellie texted me and asked if we could hang out. She'd had a really bad fight with her stepdad."

"About what?"

"She didn't tell you?" He bites his lower lip.

"No."

He sits up, all crossed legs and poofy hair. This is how he frequently looks after our make-out sessions. "It was weird. She didn't really say anything. I mean, she came over around, like, ten. She was, like, really, really trashed, *and* she wanted to get high." He shakes his head, sighs. "She was a fucking train wreck. When she finally did talk about it, it didn't make much sense."

"Well, make it make as much sense as you can." It's a lot to ask. When Ellie crossed the line of *not exactly there*, interpreting what she thought or felt was nearly impossible.

"Well . . . I'm not trying to be creepers, but did you ever notice that Ellie could be weird with her stepdad?" Tommy asks.

"Like how?" My voice is casual, but inside, my stomach twists into a knot.

"Well, like . . . um . . . you know . . . kind of flirty."

"Yeah," I say slowly. I had witnessed this before, but I'd told myself it was because she was drunk. That she was just being Ellie, pushing the boundaries as far as she could.

"I guess he finally freaked out on her, said she was trying to ruin his marriage and maybe it'd be better for everyone if she went to live with her dad."

"Wait . . . what?" I sit up, holding the blanket to my chest.

"I know." He slides up the bed frame, stretching out his long legs. He looks out the window, like he's thinking about things. I follow his gaze. When I look back at him, he's biting his thumbnail—really ripping into it.

"Stop!" I pull his hand from his mouth. The skin is raw. He looks at me. His eyes are watery. "Hey." I move closer. I hold his hand in my hand. "What's going on?"

"You don't know, then?" He glances around the room like he's taking in everything: the mashed-up sheets, his rumpled shirt in the corner, and our pants, which are unbuttoned but still on.

I hesitate, unsure. . . . Finally, though, I say, "Know what?"

"I wondered but I didn't know . . . I thought . . . I thought maybe she told you but you decided to let it, you know, go . . . because of everything that happened."

"I have no clue what you're talking about." And I don't, but I can tell that whatever he's leading up to isn't good.

"Oh." Tommy presses my hands to his bare chest, but I resist. I put them back in my lap.

"Hey, come here."

"What should I know, Tommy?" I ask firmly.

He starts biting his nail again. This time his skin tears open and starts to bleed.

"Crap, Tommy." I grab a box of Kleenex from my dresser and hand it to him. He wraps the thin sheet around his thumb, the blood like a shadow pushing through.

"That night," he says, "we got really drunk—"

"You already said that—"

"Just give a me a sec, okay, Sarah? Just . . ." He starts pacing the room, working on his other thumb. I watch, trying to figure it out, and then it's done. I know. And inside, that ball of anxiety that's been building in my belly becomes this shaky thing that bounces around. He stares at me, the tears cresting.

"You slept with her," I say slowly. "Right?" My voice rises. "That's it. Right?"

Again, he nods. "I thought that fight we had . . . It was so bad, and you said you were done with me—"

"Yeah? I've said that like a thousand times—"

"Sarah, *c'mon*! You said this time was different. *You said* you couldn't stand to look at me anymore! Don't say that's not true," he pleads. He sits down, grips my shoulders.

I push him away. The last thing I want is any part of him touching me. "We *are* done."

"Sarah, you've never wanted me to be your boyfriend. . . ." His torn-up hand circles my biceps, but I continue to resist. He squeezes my arm, says, "Stop, just listen to me—"

"Let me go." I dig my nails into his wrist, pushing so hard I'm convinced I'll break skin here, too.

"God!" He stands, looking at the half-moon imprints. "Don't be like this. We weren't hooking up anymore. I thought . . . *Sarah*, don't act like you don't have things you don't tell me! We all have secrets."

I slide back against the headboard. I pull a pillow protectively in front of me. "I've never kept a secret from you or Ellie."

We both know this is a lie. We both know I've hidden things about Jake. But Tommy's never brought that up, and he doesn't do it now, either. He comes around the bed, takes my chin in his hand, and forces me to look at him. "Sarah, please don't be like this. Don't ruin this. You and me—this is all that's left." He holds my stare. "It's not like you love me, right? Not like that." He waits. When I don't respond, he squeezes my chin.

"Tommy, you're hurting me." I try to pull away, but I can't, because he's getting worked up again, and when he's worked up, it's never good. "Please, Tommy," I say gently. "You should go. My mom's going to be home soon."

But he doesn't seem to care about that. He says, "Just say it, Sarah. Just say it."

"What? I don't know what you want me to say!"

"That you don't care about . . ." He struggles for a moment, his deep breaths filling the room. "That you've never—"

"Tommy, please!" And then I'm crying. And it's my tears that do the trick. Finally he lets me go, and I scoot to the far corner of the bed as fast as I can. "I don't know what you want from me." My voice washes away. I stare at the ceiling. I go somewhere else in my head. I see another Tommy. The one who's been my friend since the sixth grade. The second guy I ever kissed, as an experiment in Ellie's basement when I was thirteen. And, when I was fourteen, the first guy who ever held me—even if it was because I was so freaked out on acid that I thought the sirens from my sister's toy police car were actual sirens and the police were coming to take us away. And, when I was fifteen, the first guy I ever fell asleep with, even if it was because we were too drunk to move from Ellie's bedroom floor. I see *that* Tommy, not this one. And suddenly I hear him crying. And I feel sad for him. I feel so incredibly sad for us both.

I don't know what to do to make it better, but I know that he needs me. So I wrap myself around him. And even though I told him to leave, I now tell him to stay. That we'll be okay. His shoulders slump forward. He's sobbing so hard he's shaking.

A few minutes later, the sound of my mother's car fills the driveway. Tommy stiffens. He stands, grabs his shirt from the corner, and then moves toward the window. He says in a small voice, "I'm sorry, okay. I'm sorry."

I say, "I know," and then I start to straighten up the bedroom. And I tell myself to forget this afternoon, to forget that we can be this way.

5.

Let's hold hands
and pretend together.

Jake
BEFORE. NOVEMBER.

Ellie said, "It's hard for me here." It was difficult for me to understand her over the phone. Her breath was labored, so her voice shook.

I said, "What's hard for you?" It was late, real late. I had classes the next day, but I was up, I never went to sleep before three or four in the morning. "Wait," I said, and then I leaned across Amber—this girl I'd met a few days before in a bar near school—to turn down the music. "Okay, go on."

She said, "I'm struggling, Jake. It's hard for me." I wasn't surprised by the panic in her voice. Ellie had called religiously since I left Ohio. Some nights she sounded anxious, like she was afraid of being in that house without me. Other nights our conversations were fueled by her manic energy. But then there were the nights when we'd sit in near silence, the conversation having the stop-and-go rhythm of a drive filled with speed bumps. But even on those nights she was reluctant to get off the phone.

Always, she asked questions. *What did you do today? Do you still hate that teacher? Is that dude on your floor still acting like a douche?* But if I tried to ask more specific questions about her life, she'd remain silent.

"Jake, I want to come live with you," she said finally. This wasn't a new topic for us. Ellie had been pushing this idea for months, but I was reluctant. I had found control, confidence, and security in New York. My predictable routine was comforting: eight a.m. morning alarm, nine a.m. catch up on reading, ten a.m. coffee, back-to-back classes followed by homework sessions in the library. When I was lonely, I'd venture out to a bar—some place that wouldn't question my fake ID—to meet girls whose names I'd soon forget. For the first time in my life, I was completely selfish, and I liked it. I felt the weight of responsibility for my mother and sister lift. I felt the rising emotions that often accompany hope. I felt free. "It's only a week until Thanksgiving break. Can we discuss it then?"

Ellie said, "Jake, I think I really need to come now."

I turned on my side and stared at the black-and-white Jim Morrison poster Sarah had given to me the night before I left. I thought about the inscription on the back, a loose reference to one of my favorite Doors songs: *I don't know what's on the other side of all this, but I hope one day you'll take me there.*

"Come on, Ellie," I said, knowing I had already stepped to the other side and found a solitude there that could not coexist with her or my mom or Sarah.

Amber nudged me. "Who's Ellie?"

"My sister. It's my sister."

She rolled onto her belly, the blanket covering her from the waist down. I traced the outline of her ribs with my index finger. She looked at me, possessively. "I didn't know you had a sister."

Ellie's voice deepened an octave, which is how she always sounded when she became defensive. "Who's that? Are you there with someone? Jake? I want to talk to you alone. Why don't you ever fucking know how to be alone?"

I said to Amber, "Hey, can you give me a second?"

She narrowed her eyes. I nudged her with my foot. *Just a second,* I mouthed, and finally she moved, taking the outline of her ribs with her. In the bathroom, she propped open the window and lit up. She perched on the toilet seat cover, balancing effortlessly, like a bird on a wire.

"Is she gone?" Ellie asked.

"Yeah."

"Good." Ellie paused. "Jake, I just want to come live with you now. You don't know what it's like for me. How hard it can be . . . Everything is . . ."

Amber coughed. I turned to look at her. She smiled, slipped a hand down her breast and rib cage, and rested it flat across her pelvis, the fingertips pointed downward, just barely brushing her—

"Jake?" Ellie said.

Often when Ellie was drunk or high or popped too many of our mother's prescription pills, she sounded paranoid. "Hey, when was the last time you slept?"

"Jake, come on, please don't do that." Her voice rose. "This is serious. I need to talk to you . . . in person." She started to cry then, a deep shuddering cry filled with wild breaths and hiccups.

"Hey. Hey, now, tell me. Why can't you tell me now?"

Ellie was crying too hard to answer. I glanced at Amber, struggling to keep my distance from my sister's drama, from the request I knew was coming.

"I just can't," she said finally. "Not over the phone. You said if I needed you, Jake, you'd come. So come home."

I sighed, remembering my promise. My thoughts moved to the amount of time it would take to drive home to Ohio and what I would need to do: pack, send e-mails to teachers, rent a car. I thought about the slick roads and the snowbanks piled high from an early-November storm. Again, I thought about my mom and Sarah.

"Jake, you promised."

"Yeah, I promised."

"You'll come?"

"Yeah, as soon as I can."

"Okay, that's good." She stayed silent for a few minutes. Her breaths evened out, settling into a quieter rise and fall. Then the phone went silent, and I knew she was gone.

For a few minutes I sat with my cell cradled in my palm. Then I went to the closet, grabbed a few shirts and an extra pair of jeans to throw into my duffel bag. I added underwear, socks, and shoes. In the bathroom I grabbed my toothbrush. All the while, Amber watched. Still perched on the toilet. Still naked. Still smoking, her eyes glassed over.

She said, "Hey . . ."

"Hey . . ." I touched her nipple, fascinated by its walnut-like color. She smiled and took a hit from her pipe. Her other hand stroked my leg.

She said, "You gotta go? Already?"

"Yeah, I should."

She said, "Now? Tonight?"

"Yeah, I really should. It's a long drive, about eleven hours to Ohio, and I have to rent a car . . ."

Her hand stroked higher.

"Tonight? Really? It's too late to drive tonight."

"Yeah, but I should go."

She put her pipe down and said, "Not tonight. There's too much ice on the roads." And then she stopped talking, her breath suddenly warm against my thigh. Her glossy black hair swung back and forth like a curtain ruffled by a fan. "Besides, you'll never find a rental place open this late. No," she repeated, "not tonight."

A few seconds later her breath was still warm against my thigh, and I said, "It'd be crazy to drive in the dark." And then, a few more seconds after that, "I'll leave tomorrow, after classes."

She turned her head upward, running her tongue across her lips. Her dark brown eyes reminded me of Sarah's, but I chased those thoughts away. I didn't want to think about Sarah or Tommy or going back there. I just wanted to get lost in Amber and the moment. She said, "Tomorrow night is best."

She was right. The roads were icy. And what good would I be to Ellie if I got into a car wreck? And I told myself, *Ellie is tough.*

Ellie can make it one more day. Sarah and Tommy will watch over her. She'll be okay.

And then I said, "Yeah, tomorrow night."

She led the way back to bed, her glossy black hair skimming her olive-colored butt. She reached for the light, but I pushed her hand away. I wanted to see everything. She smiled at me. I thought, *One more day won't matter. She'll be fine.*

Amber climbed on top of me, and when she did, I didn't think about Ellie anymore.

6.

In the bathroom, with my
hair still dripping wet, I'd
devise a plan. First, towel-
dry quickly. Second, put on
underwear and declare that
place safe. Next, tank top,
socks, then pj's. Declare
those places safe too. And
then tiptoe to the bedroom,
lock the door behind me,
declare my room safe.

In the morning, try not to
remember why.

Jessie
AFTER. JANUARY.

After Lola leaves, I sit on my bed and stare at the wall until I notice the tiniest sliver of paint flaking off. It's the smallest imperfection, but for some reason it breaks my heart.

We painted this room five years ago, just a few short months after moving to Smith. Sarah picked midnight blue for the walls. I picked silver for the door. Mom did most of the painting, her hips swaying to some old music by some old lady.

Later that night, the smell of paint lingered in the air. Sarah rolled onto her side, pulled her brown hair into a ponytail, and said, with serious eyes, "Mom was so weird today, but in, like, a good way. Like all that dancing? She seemed almost . . ." She didn't say "happy" or "relaxed"—although either of those words would have been right—because back then we didn't think about our parents' inner lives. But when their behavior was unusual, we noticed.

"What kind of necklace was she was wearing?" I thought back to the bright blue stone resting against her collarbone, a recent gift from my dad. The color was nearly the same as her eyes, and it made them appear even brighter.

"Turquoise," Sarah murmured. And then, because she had a habit of repeating words she liked, she said it again, only with less force. I followed her lead, repeating the word twice, the second time a perfect imitation of her.

"Do you want to play glamour dolls tomorrow?" Sarah asked. Before she met Ellie and became popular, Sarah spent hours hiding behind her bed, building a glamour-doll city. I preferred daydreaming or reading books that were a bit too advanced for me, like *Forever* by Judy Blume. I'd found a worn copy in Mom's memory chest, read it as fast as I could, and felt sad for weeks after because it taught me that boys were gross and first love didn't last forever.

"I don't know." I pretended to consider the question, enjoying her having to ask me for something for a change.

"Please. It's fun."

And sometimes it was, but sometimes it felt oddly routine. The story lines were always about some popular girl struck by tragedy. Her father disappears. Sister gets kidnapped. Mom up and runs away. There were rarely happy endings.

I told Ellie about this a month before she died. It was October. The fireflies had already burrowed their blinking bodies away for a long winter, but inside Ellie's bedroom it was nice and warm. "Makes sense to me," she said. "Where'd her real dad go, anyways?"

Maybe this connection should have been obvious to me. I was always looking for connections, always searching for answers, always wondering why.

Like, why do fireflies have lights that blink on and off?

Answer: They're trying to attract a mate.

But just as I had never questioned my mother's happiness, I had never thought to question Sarah's place in our family or wonder if that somehow made her feel different.

I didn't want us to be anything less than we were, but the truth of what Ellie said was hard to ignore. Sarah's brown eyes and olive skin were a sharp contrast to our blue eyes and milky complexions. Sarah could effortlessly reach the upper shelves in the kitchen, while the rest of us, Dad excluded, needed to climb onto the counters. The dividing lines, which had always existed, were suddenly filled in. She was my half sister, but I didn't want her to be that. I didn't want her to be anything but whole.

• • •

At school Lola grips my arm tightly and guides me slowly through the crowded halls. When we pass a shy alternative girl with green streaks in her hair, Lola says loudly, "That is so not a good look for you." Then turns to me and adds, "Oh my God. Did you see that? That girl's a freak show."

Ever since Lola's parents split last February, she's been getting worse. That's when her mom started saying things like, *How many times do I have to tell you to turn off the lights? God, Lola, is anyone home in there?* And her dad stopped coming around. And her older brother had moved out because he couldn't take their parents fighting. And now Lola is a lot meaner to everybody. Like right now, when I actually bump into something, she snaps, "How many times do I have to tell you? Nobody's staring at you!"

We stop at our lockers. I undo my combination lock and peel off my layers. I keep my scarf wrapped around my neck because it's so cold in the hallways. Even my long sleeves and thick sweater don't keep me warm.

"Oh, please, Jess, you're not wearing that. You look like you have no neck." Lola snatches my scarf and tosses it into her locker. "There." She leans against the metal. "That's better . . . *Oh, look.*" Her eyes narrow. She points across the hall.

It's Tommy, his arm casually draped across some blond freshman with jagged gray eyeliner and matching skintight jeans. Lola sighs loudly. "What does he see in her?"

"Don't know," I say, even though her slightness, pale skin, and light hair instantly remind me of Ellie.

"Isn't he still seeing your sister?" Lola's tone is sour.

"No clue." I haven't liked Tommy since he called me annoying at Sarah's twelfth birthday party and continued to be mean to me until I grew boobs. That's when he started playing nice, and I realized he was one of those guys who is never kind unless he wants something from you.

Lola must realize Tommy's fascination with boobs; she arches her back against her locker, her breasts protruding like ready-to-launch rockets. "Hey, Tommy."

"Hey, Lola." Tommy smiles, whispers something into the blond girl's ear, and just like that she disappears. She's barely gone before he turns to stare at Lola's sweater. "Come on," he says, then walks away. He doesn't look back to see if she's following, but Lola is unfazed. She smiles triumphantly at me, tosses her bag into her locker, and slams the door shut.

"Lola," I say, "he's walking in the wrong direction. Mrs. Medina's class is this way." But Lola either doesn't hear me or doesn't care, because she's half skipping, half running after him.

Now I am alone in the hallway. I undo Lola's combination lock, grab my scarf, and wrap it protectively around my neck. Then I stand there, feeling slightly paralyzed. This panic is always worse in the morning. It's something about all these people shoving and pushing, their backpacks full and eyes half open as they rush to first-period classes, that makes me feel like there's less oxygen here.

Still, I have to get to class, so I start walking slowly, my eyes glued to the linoleum floor.

Somewhere near the classroom, a warm hand touches my arm. At first I think it's Lola, but the hand is too gentle. I raise my eyes. Clara Lee, our sophomore-class president, is standing beside me. We're not really friends, but I've known her since middle school. She smiles. I try to smile back, but it doesn't work, so I shrug my shoulders, and say, "Hey . . ."

"Hey!" she says. "Going to Mrs. Medina's class?"

I nod, and she slips her arm through mine. "If we don't hustle, we're going to be late!" she says. And then we're moving briskly through the halls. The final bell rings as we cross the classroom's threshold. Clara releases my arm and says, "That was close!"

I sit down at my desk. Behind me, Lola's seat is empty. Mrs. Medina writes on the dry-erase board. Her fingers are quick and hypnotic. Watching her makes me tired. I put my head down, twirl my pen, and think about the things that change us. Maybe the divorce and what Tommy did to Lola last summer changed her? Maybe what happened between Ellie and me changed me, too?

The second tardy bell rings. Mrs. Medina takes attendance. When she asks why Lola isn't in class, I pretend I don't hear.

7.

This emptiness . . .

Sarah
FIVE YEARS BEFORE.

Our worlds collided on my twelfth birthday. One minute I was running home from middle school, backpack banging furiously against my shoulders, and the next I was lying in a heap on Mr. Lumpnick's yard, textbooks and papers scattered around me. By the time I looked up, she was already standing above me, pulling leaves out of her blond hair.

"What the fuck?" she said, and kicked me lightly with her shoe. "Seriously? Why the eff don't you watch where you're going?"

She was just a scrawny girl with stringy blond hair and orb-like blue eyes, and it took a few seconds for me to accept that I had hit her and not something much larger, like a car or a tree.

"I'm s-sorry," I stuttered, pulling myself to my knees. "I didn't see you." This was true. When I'd cut the corner of our block, I had been too busy thinking about other things—my birthday party's to-do list, that new outfit I'd wear, my elaborate fantasy of how this party would change my very unpopular life—to notice insignificant details like who was standing in the middle of the normally empty sidewalk.

"Well, you should watch where you're going," she repeated.

Well, you should watch where you're standing, I thought, but didn't dare say that out loud. Politeness was a big deal in my family. But obviously not in hers, from the way she stared at me as I gathered my things.

I zipped up my bag, only then realizing my left hand was empty. The birthday balloons my mom had had delivered to the school—the ones that had made the mean-girl patrol stare at me with envy—were gone. I sank back onto the grass, feeling mostly defeated.

"It's your birthday?" she asked.

I lifted my head. "How'd you know?"

She pointed mysteriously to the sky, where the balloons hovered above us, caught in a bright explosion of golden leaves. She jumped up, catching the tiniest thread of ribbon between her fingers. She gave a firm tug, and the balloons shot downward, popping with a sudden hiss on the tree's sharp branches.

"Here." She handed me the deflated corpses. "It's my birthday too. Well, tomorrow." She tossed blond hairs out of her eyes.

"Oh," I said, my eyes moving between her and the dead balloons.

"Yeah, weird, huh?" She kicked me again with her shoe. "Are you just going to sit there all day?"

I stood, pulled my bag onto my shoulders, and tried to brush the mud and grass off my jeans. I began to walk toward home, the dead balloons dragging behind me. She followed.

"So, are you having a party?"

"Yep" was all I said, until she nudged me with her elbow. Then I added, "At six. You?"

"No." She picked a blade of grass from my hair and handed it to me. "My mom's going through this thing. This bad divorce thing, so I think she forgot or something." She shrugged her shoulders like it wasn't a big deal, but I could tell it was. My mom never forgot birthdays. Right then she was probably in our yellow kitchen, cooking my favorite birthday dinner—pot roast and twice-baked potatoes.

"That sucks, but, listen . . ." I pointed toward my house. "I gotta, you know . . ." I started up my walkway, but it wasn't long before I heard the sound of crushed leaves behind me. Seconds later, she stood once again in my path.

"Hey, can I come to your party?"

"Huh?" I avoided eye contact, hoping she'd get the hint, but when I finally looked back at her, she was still waiting expectantly. I coughed and said, "I mean, I would, but . . ."

She looked away then, her shoulders rising up and down the way Jessie's did when she was embarrassed. "Oh, yeah. I totally get it. I've just been gone all summer with this thing between my mom and stepdad, but my brother told me about your family moving in and, you know, he said you were cool. . . . And I just thought since we, like, live right there . . ." She pointed across the street toward a green ranch-style home, where a boy with a pitch-black faux hawk sat, smoking a cigarette.

"Wait. That's where you live? That's your brother?" Even if Mom called him a punk, he was still the most sought-after boy in the neighborhood. That was probably because he was seriously beautiful, with the darkest blue eyes I'd ever seen.

She eyed me warily. "Yeah."

I placed a hand to my lower belly, where an unfamiliar tingling sensation had begun.

"Why are you smiling?"

I straightened my lips. "I'm—I'm not. I—I was just thinking that you should come."

"Yeah?" Her blue eyes lit up.

"Yeah, and . . ." I shifted nervously. "Why don't you bring your brother, too?"

She smiled as if she'd almost expected this. "What about Tommy? He lives in our pool house with his mom. I go to the same private school with him this year. His mom's a secretary there, you know, but next year I'm going back to public school, just like you." She sighed, like she hated having to explain herself. "I mean, Tommy and me both, probably."

"Um, yeah. Okay." I was too busy thinking about her brother calling me cool to care about any of these details. "Just bring anybody you'd like."

Her smile grew. "Thanks. What's your name?"

"Sarah," I said. "What's yours?"

She shoved more blond hairs from her eyes. "I'm Ellie, and that," she said, glancing back at her house, "is Jake."

A few hours later, Jess twirled around the basement, her blue-and-yellow skirt blending into one big rainbow that made me feel dizzy and happy at the same time. The party had started thirty minutes earlier, but still there was no sign of Ellie or Jake.

Jess stopped spinning long enough to tighten her pigtails and stare suspiciously at the crowded basement. "Did Mom say you could have this many guests?"

I gave her a look. Popularity at Smith Middle didn't come with a little sister attached, especially one who acted like a goody-goody. "Jess, come on. It's totally lame for you to be here. And Mom already told you. Okay?"

The doorbell rang. Jess's head shot up. Mom had specifically asked her to be the doorman tonight so that she would feel included but be kept occupied upstairs. "But you'll tell me everything tonight?"

"Promise." I nudged her forward. "Go."

Alone again, I counted heads, trying hard to ignore the possibility that Jake was about to walk down my stairs. Twenty-seven kids were present. Some of them popular, like Billy Mancuso, who had the best dimpled smile, and Vanessa Gomez, who was probably the prettiest girl in our class, and Tori Levitts, who was her much taller and not-so-pretty best friend.

It was hard not to wonder why they had come to my party. So far life at Smith Middle had consisted of my randomly walking up to groups of kids and hovering awkwardly, or lurking around campus feeling lonely and embarrassed.

It was that desperation and my mom's suggestion that I *try harder* that led to my having a birthday party. My father said to aim high with the guest list, *because why not?* So I wrote out seventeen invitations, inviting the more popular kids, while never actually believing they'd show up. But here they were—along with ten other kids I hadn't invited—and many had set down colorfully wrapped boxes on the gift table.

I should have been happy, but I wasn't. Nobody had really talked to me except, oddly, to ask when Ellie would arrive. Twenty-seven kids in my basement, and I still had zero friends.

Suddenly the basement door opened. The kitchen light crept down the stairs, pooling around my feet. Above, Jess's ponytails swung with excitement. "You got more guests!" she sang dramatically.

Three bodies pushed passed her, the light like bright halos above their heads. Ellie, dressed in tight blue hip-hugging jeans and a perfectly faded *Mork & Mindy* T-shirt, led the way downstairs. Another kid trailed behind her, a goofy grin on his face. Jake followed, in skinny jeans, a frayed T-shirt that barely fit, and his trademark pout.

Everyone stopped talking. The music seemed to fade. I opened my mouth, but before I could speak, Jess sang out in that soprano voice of hers, "Mom wants to talk to you! Now!"

Behind me, a handful of people snickered.

"Does she always sing everything like that? It's *annoying*," the kid with Ellie sang back, and everyone but Jess, who quickly moved away from the doorway, laughed.

"She gets really excited," I said, halfheartedly defending her.

He handed me a daisy wet with dew. "Happy birthday, *Sar-rah*," he said, dragging out my name in a squeaky voice that may have belonged to him or some ironic version of a character he was playing.

"That's Tommy," Ellie said, shoving him. "And this"—Ellie handed me a simple brown box with my name written across the top in bright purple calligraphy—"is from me and Jake." She nudged her brother with her elbow.

"Yeah," Jake muttered. He rubbed the bottom of his eye, smearing some of his kohl eyeliner.

"What is it?" I asked, shaking the box.

Ellie's face lit up. "It's a *Happy Days* T-shirt. Jake found it and some other cool stuff"—she pointed to her own T-shirt—"last week on the curb in front of Old Mrs. Sawyer's house. What a waste. Right?"

"Oh . . . ," I said, not quite sure how to react to a gift picked out of a garbage can. I glanced around, and realized everyone was staring at us—Tori going so far as to wave at Jake, who simply averted his eyes.

"Do you like *Happy Days*?" Ellie asked.

"I bet she's never heard of it," Tommy scoffed.

"Who hasn't?" I said, although I hadn't, and walked a few

feet away to place the box and daisy on the gift table.

"Don't worry about them," Ellie said, following me. She eyed the other kids, smiling indulgently at Tori. "They always do that when we're around. I forgot to tell you. We're kind of *it*." She picked up the daisy, tucked it behind my ear, and led me back to Jake and Tommy. We formed a circle, me standing stiffly between Jake and Ellie. I noticed I was the same height as him. Clearly, I told myself, a sign from God we were destined to be together.

"Cool party, I guess." Ellie looked around the room. "If you like these people."

Jess's singsong voice floated downstairs again. *"Now, Sarah!"*

Reluctantly, I headed for the stairs, trying my best to imitate Ellie's casual stride, knowing that these matters—annoying sisters and overconcerned mothers—would never disturb someone like her. Jess waited for me on the kitchen landing.

"How's it going?" she asked, twirling her hair.

"Do you have to be so annoying?" I snapped, and her face fell.

"Sarah . . ." Mom sat at the kitchen table, nervously drinking a cup of tea. "Be nice to your sister."

"Mom, she's completely embarrassing me."

"I'm not," Jess said.

"Yes, you are!"

"Jess. Sarah." Mom's voice was stern. We both quieted down.

After a second she said, "Sarah, I know I encouraged you to have this party, but some of these kids are making me uncomfortable."

She looked at me like she always did—first with worry, then with disappointment. She began giving me this face when I was seven and convinced Jess she could fly, which left my sister with a small scar above her right eye.

Mom touched her stomach, which was the size of a basketball, and yawned. "I can't really go up and down those stairs anymore. They're too steep, and your father doesn't want me to do anything that might hurt Mattie."

Two nights before, I had overheard my parents discussing what would happen after Mattie was born. Mom wanted to get her tubes tied, but Dad said one day they'd try for a boy. Mom said, "I don't care if I have a boy, Glenn. I'm done."

It was weird to hear my parents argue, and even weirder to think Dad might love us less because we were girls, and maybe me least of all because, technically, I wasn't even his girl.

"Have you heard a word I said?" Mom asked now.

My expression said *Of course I heard you,* when in fact I had not. "Mom, everyone's okay downstairs. Nothing's happening," I reassured her.

Mom shook her head. It was a typical Mom move. Sometimes I'd find her in the kitchen, washing dishes, shaking her head at absolutely nobody. "I don't know, Sarah." She inhaled sharply, and winced as if the baby had kicked her. "Just be good. Don't do anything stupid, okay?"

"Okay," I said sullenly. "Promise."

She sighed and gave me a new look, one that said she wanted to tell me a thousand different things but knew that not one of them—her intuitive mom feelings—could be said in a language I might understand.

Downstairs, Jake leaned next to a propped-open basement window, smoking a cigarette and watching the others like he was watching the Discovery Channel. Nearby, Ellie was being courted by a group of giggling girls, which included Tori and Vanessa. She watched me descend the stairs, waving me over with an empty bottle. "Play?" she asked when I got close enough. I saw Tori and Vanessa exchange a knowing smile.

"What?"

Ellie laughed. She walked to the center of the room and placed the bottle on the floor, directly beneath the spinning disco lights. Eventually, she got everyone to form a misshapen circle.

It wasn't long before the bottle was spun several times and newly formed couples disappeared into the bathroom, laundry room, and supply closet for seven minutes in heaven.

When it was Jake's turn to spin the bottle, I held my breath—willing, wishing, praying, even—as the glass revolved three times before clearly landing on me. Jake shrugged and stood up. I followed him, pressing myself against the wall to let the departing couple pass as we took over the laundry room.

"Forget something?" he asked. I turned around to twenty-five pairs of eyes watching us.

"Oh." I shut the door, and I sat opposite him on the floor. Jake leaned back against the wall. We studied each other for a minute before he spoke.

"What do you think?" he asked. He leaned forward, and his breath curled around my nostrils, hints of cigarette and peppermint.

"About . . . ?" The question caught me off guard.

"About this. Your party."

"It's good," I said, my voice trembling from the anxiety of being alone in a room with him. "Are you . . . are you having fun?"

He shrugged, picking at a tear in his T-shirt. The hole grew wider until I could see a sliver of his pale flesh. "I'm not really into crowds," he said, with a small smile. "But Ellie wanted to come."

There was an uncomfortable silence, and he said, "I guess I should kiss you. If that's cool?"

I nodded, and we locked eyes for a second, my breath caught in my throat. He pulled me to my knees and, with his hands on my hips, slid me toward him until our pelvises touched. Then he studied my face, his eyes slowly moving from the width of my forehead to the dip in my chin.

Suddenly, his lips were on mine, his tongue gently pushing my mouth open. I closed my eyes, the world spinning around me, until nothing remained but his lips on my lips and his hands firm and warm against my back.

8.

It was as simple as telling you how it's done. Press harder. It'll hurt at first, but doesn't everything hurt at first? And didn't you say you wanted a tattoo one day? That will hurt too. Remember when I taught you to smoke? You coughed and you said your lungs ached. This will ache like that, only more. But you know what I didn't tell you? The thing that hurts the most is that my mom will never ask me why my arms are bandaged, why my forearms are covered in all this scarred flesh. And the other thing that hurts is that I know I'll never be able to press the whole way down. That I'll always be stuck wanting to push through but too afraid to try.

Jake

AFTER. NOVEMBER.

After Mom finishes crying, she asks me to bring her a Valium
from her nightstand. The gold curtains are drawn in her bedroom. I remember how Ellie and I hid behind that swell of fabric, quietly playing Go Fish, happy to have outsmarted Mom's
Saturday chore list.

That was when our father was still around, when Ellie was
learning to ride my Spider-Man Big Wheel and I had upgraded
to a BMX with training wheels. That was when Mom came
home wearing scrubs, the smell of hospital still on her white
doctor's coat, and Dad set his briefcase next to the door, keys
on the kitchen counter. That was when Saturdays were for
taming our suburban lawn. When Dad, sweat dripping from

the tips of his ash-brown hair, massacred the blooming wild-flowers that grew around the picket fence Mom had made him install when I was four. That was when Dad asked for my help, and I gathered the colorful buds into a bouquet I gave to Ellie.

Mom's room is particularly tidy, an act of an uneasy mind. It's easy to find the pill bottle on the nightstand. I let it roll down my palm and across my fingertips, then back. I twist the top and, out of habit, survey the contents. The three remaining pills, settled near the bottom, are obscured by the body of a gold key. I know without question this is the key to Ellie's bedroom.

"Jake?" Mom calls from the other room. I shove the key into my pocket and shake a Valium into my palm. I stop in the kitchen to grab a glass of water.

"Here." I hand her the pill and the water. Then I extend my hand for her empty glass. "You should lie down for a bit. Rest." I grab an afghan from the armchair, wrap it around her shoulders, and tuck her graying hair behind her ears.

Mom gazes at the room. Her eyes move past the Ethan Allen furniture she bought with Sargeant after they were married and the 1920s bookcase she inherited from her dad, and stop at the liquor cabinet. She says, "We never said don't drink. We just said don't drink too much. And don't drive when you're drunk. And don't be stupid. But we never said don't do it at all. I guess that was the wrong thing to do. Wasn't it, Jake?"

"Oh, Mom." I sit beside her. I feel weighed down by her guilt, and my guilt too. "Stop it. Stop torturing yourself. Why are you doing this?" I circle my arms around her. Tell myself that in this moment she is safe. "We can sell the place. You can move south to the Carolinas or something. You hate winters. Right?"

She is sobbing. "I should have never kept those pills in the house. I should have known better . . . with her . . ." She buries her head in the crook of my arm. "You don't think . . ." And it's that thought again, the one she's been trying to express for days. The one we keep wondering about but don't say out loud.

"It was an accident," I reassure her. "You know how she was . . . This time it just got the best of her." I don't tell her about the phone call. I don't tell her it was my fault.

She says, "I can't live here anymore."

"You don't have to, Mom. Okay? We'll figure it out." I rub her back before settling her down onto the sofa. I crouch beside her, give her my hand. She pulls it to her breastbone and holds on tightly. I stay there until she falls asleep.

• • •

Mom once said her father was the stereotypical Irish policeman, a heavy drinker with a heavy hand, but Ellie and I never knew him. He died of a heart attack before Mom finished her last year of medical school. Our grandmother had died of ovarian cancer fifteen years before that, when Mom was just eleven.

Once, when I was eleven, I told Mom she shouldn't date. That Dad wouldn't like it. That he would never come back to us if she kept having boyfriend after boyfriend. She said, "He's not coming back. And if this is the worst thing I do to you, then you're lucky. Believe me, you don't know how bad a parent can be." And I did believe her. Even then I knew there were worse things a mother could do than have too many boyfriends and drink the weekend away. A mother could die and leave you behind, defenseless in a crazy world.

After Mom is asleep, I wander the house, thinking about these things—the family histories that shape us from generation to generation—and, eventually, I find myself standing outside Ellie's bedroom. I take the key from my pocket, unlock the door, and, from the threshold, survey the interior: Ellie's neatly made bed shoved against the wall. The CDs piled on her desk—a combination of emo, punk, folk, and bluegrass bands. The photos taped to the bookshelf, windowsills, and desk, taken with the Polaroid camera I found Dumpster-diving last year.

The room smells like vinegar and vanilla-scented candles. I remember that morning, finding Jessie down on her knees, scrubbing the wood floor clean. I wonder why she would do that. But then that thought is gone, taken over by the question Mom and I have been avoiding since the day we lost Ellie. The tension in my jaw returns, and I will myself to think about other things: school, helping Mom contact a Realtor, Sarah . . .

I stare out the window and think about Sarah. I wonder if she's doing better. I wonder if I should go to her. I want to tell her everything. I want to let her rub my head until it falls forward in perfect submission. But I can't. The world has shifted too much, and I don't know where to go from here.

9.

I'm convinced I could stand in the middle of the road and not be hit by a car. I am invisible. I do not exist.

Jessie

AFTER. JANUARY.

Mrs. Medina calls me to her desk after class. She waits until the room has emptied and the final bell for the next period—her planning period—has sounded before she asks about Sarah. Back when Sarah cared about school, Mrs. Medina was her favorite teacher. It's the reason why I worked so hard to get into her class.

"Jess? Did you hear my question?" Mrs. Medina clears her throat and says hesitantly, "Jess? Look at me."

"Yeah." I stare at a balled-up sheet of paper just shy of the garbage can for a few seconds, and then I force my eyes to hers. Her gaze is so reassuring it unnerves me.

"It's okay," she says. "You're not in trouble."

"I know." I stare at her blankly.

"Do you?" she asks, but we both know this is a rhetorical question. "Look, Jess, you're doing a fantastic job given the circumstances, but you're so quiet in class. You used to talk before . . ."

The dot-dot-dot is standard speak around me now. When your very popular sister has accidentally overdosed and unenrolled from school, people tend to ask you questions with the dot-dot-dot attached. So the silence that follows isn't as uncomfortable for me as it is for Mrs. Medina.

"Jessie, I'm worried about you." She presses a hand to her neck and pauses to consider her words. "Maybe I should have a conversation with your mom—"

"No! Please, Mrs. Medina, don't."

Mrs. Medina raises her eyebrows. I've never exclaimed anything to her before.

"It's just my mom . . ." I stop to take a deep breath. "My mom's going through a lot, and I don't want her to worry."

This is true. Lately, Mom's hands are more nervous than ever. I want to take them into my own and say, *Please just be still.* But I know that won't help. So I try hard not to add to her stress, by being extra careful with my responsibilities at home and at school.

"But what are *you* going through?" Mrs. Medina says. The

question seems obvious, but she's the first to ask it since everything fell apart.

"I'm fine." I slip my eyes downward, toward the crumpled paper. I wonder if it is a love note someone dropped by mistake or a blank sheet discarded only because it was torn. The latter possibility seems unbearable.

Mrs. Medina's hand slides forward like she's reaching for me.

"I'm fine," I repeat, and her hand slides back. She sets it on her hip and waits. I wait too.

Finally, she says, "Okay, Jess. If that's how you really feel . . ."

It takes some doing, but I give her the confidence stare, the one that makes teachers believe you know the answer to any question they might ask. In return Mrs. Medina offers a kind but concerned smile. She says, "Okay, Jess, you can go for now."

At her door she hands me a hall pass and sighs. I carry the weight of her breath for a long while.

BEFORE. JULY.

I didn't understand what Meg was saying when she burst into my bedroom, shouting. I just knew that Meg was being Meg and I was being me.

Meg was eleven, slightly tomboyish, and happy to fight

about everything from sparkly stickers to bike horns. My mom often called her "the little shouter," and it wasn't unusual for her to fly into a room, excited about something.

It was Saturday, which according to Lola was pedicure day, and even with the sudden disruption her steady fingers still moved swiftly across her toes. "Meg, just go and play with your Barbies, okay?" she murmured, without looking up.

"I don't play with Barbies," Meg said, but the whole Barbie world set up in the corner of our basement said otherwise.

"God, do something about this already, Jess." Lola gave me a look that usually meant that I had done something wrong, even if that something was not doing anything at all.

"Come on, Meg." I picked up a pillow and tossed it lightly at her head.

"Hey!" She dodged the pillow, a hurt expression spreading across her face. "It's my house too!"

"But not your room," Lola said.

"Fine. I'll just go watch Sarah *make out* with Tommy by myself, then."

There was a bit of silence. It was the first time either of us had heard about Sarah and Tommy. I glanced at Lola. She looked as shocked as I felt. Meg, guessing she had revealed a really juicy secret, let her smile grow until it covered half her face.

Lola spoke first. Her voice sounded almost calm, but I could hear the underlying tremble. "You're lying."

Meg's smile faltered. "No, I'm not."

Lola shot off the bed and partly waddled, partly hopped over to Meg. "You're lying!" she said again. Meg took a step back, her entire body shrinking inward.

"I—I'm not," she stammered. "I'm not." She looked to me, then back to Lola, her mouth hanging partially open.

Lola snapped her fingers in front of Meg's face. "Details. *Now.*"

Meg took a deep breath and began to tell us a complicated story about playing hide-and-go-seek with some of the neighborhood kids. Lola interrupted her and said, "Just get to the end."

"Well," Meg said, "I hid behind the cottage, and that's when I heard Sarah's voice, and . . ." She paused to catch her breath. "She and Tommy were totally in his room, making out!"

"Fuck me!" Lola said, and Meg's eyes grew wide. We weren't allowed to curse in the house or anywhere else.

"You can't say those words," Meg said. "Jess, tell her she can't say that."

Lola tore the cotton balls from between her toes, shoved her flip-flops on, and waved her arms at me impatiently. "What are you waiting for, Jess?"

I was waiting for her common sense to kick in, but I didn't

say that. Instead I said, "No, thanks," and looked back at my feet.

"You're going," she said.

"Nope. Sarah can make out with Tommy even if he is disgusting," I told her. "We can't just spy on them."

She gave me an intense look I couldn't quite read, grabbed my flip-flops, and shoved them into my hands. "You're going."

Once we got outside, Lola stopped in front of Jake's house and said, "We can just go through that side gate." She pointed to a path on the left side of the house and squared her shoulders like she was preparing for battle.

"Honestly, I don't get why this is such a big deal to you."

"Just come on," she said, and started toward the path, but I held steady. A second later, Meg was standing beside me.

"I want to come!" She tugged at her jeans, which had ridden up on her thighs so that her ankles stuck out awkwardly. I felt bad for her. Eleven was one of those ages where you were caught between so many phases. You were too young to stay up late, but old enough to get your period. You had to wear bras, even though you barely had boobs. And boys wanted to kiss you, not because they liked you, but because someone dared them to. But the worst part about being eleven was realizing that your older sister, the person you always considered your best friend, wasn't even your friend at all.

Lola turned back, her eyes narrowing at Meg. "Effing A, Meg. Go home. You're too young for this shit."

"I'm only four years younger than you guys," Meg protested.

"Oh, God. Jess, *please.*" Lola raised her arms in frustration.

"Meg," I said, ignoring her pleading look, "you have to go."

But Meg didn't budge, and I admired her for her toughness.

"Look at this shit," Lola muttered. She crossed toward Meg and barked meanly into her face, "Go home, you little squirt!"

Meg's eyes filled with tears. "Jess?"

I remembered the day Sarah threw me over in favor of Ellie, but I told myself that this wasn't like that. That I was sending Meg home to protect her from whatever Lola was dragging me into.

"Go on, Meg," I said.

Meg looked from Lola to me, her chin shaking. Then she turned on her heel, her awkward ankles slowly carrying her home.

Lola grabbed my arm, but I yanked it away from her. "Just wait," I said, keeping my eyes on Meg until our front door shut behind her. Then I turned to Lola and said, "Okay, let's go."

10.

What do you tell me? What
do I tell you? I feel like
there are so many things
I can't tell you. Are there
things you can't tell me? Do
you know who your father is?
Do you want to know?

I know who my father is, but
I don't <u>know</u> him at all.

Sarah

FIVE YEARS BEFORE.

"Aren't you happy we came?" Ellie asked me the night of my party. Everyone else had gone home, but Ellie stayed behind to help me clean up. Afterward, we sat on the concrete floor in the middle of my basement, the disco ball spinning fluorescent colors above us. "They worship Jake, you know. It's ridiculous," she said. She rolled up her jeans so that her ankle was exposed, and pulled off a Band-Aid, picking at the scab beneath.

"Doesn't that hurt?" I asked.

She nodded.

"Then why pick at it?"

She shrugged and ripped off a big chunk of the scab, exposing a round patch of puckered pink flesh. A surprising amount of blood started to seep out. She watched for a second, almost fascinated, and then asked for a tissue.

I returned quickly from the bathroom with a wad of toilet paper, which she pressed over the wound. "We should do something for your birthday tomorrow, even if you can't have a party," I said.

She laughed. "We just did."

"What do you mean?"

"Your party," she said. "It was my party too. Why do you think so many people showed up? And did you check out all the gifts I got?"

I stared at Ellie, wondering if she might be a little crazy. The evidence was stacked against her: She picked at scabs until they bled, kicked or nudged you whenever she felt like it, and apparently made up impossible stories. "I invited everyone that came tonight," I said slowly, before it clicked in that a good number of people I hadn't invited had also shown up. I stood up and crossed to the gift table. I picked up several gifts and flipped open the gift tabs. All but one were addressed to Ellie. "But how did you know who I invited?"

Ellie looked from the disco ball to me. "Tori and Vanessa told me. We're kind of best friends . . . except lately, I think they're totally boring." She smiled. "Nobody was coming to your party until I said we were having a joint party—"

"But you didn't even know I was having a party . . ." I felt a knot twist in my stomach.

"Vanessa told me weeks ago. I never said I didn't know about your party—"

"But you asked if I was having one—"

"But I never said I didn't *know* what your answer would be."

"It's the same thing," I protested.

"No, it's not. Anyway . . ." She smiled triumphantly. "I fixed it. So it's no big deal."

I was silent. I couldn't decide how I felt: embarrassed that nobody had wanted to come to my party; mad that Ellie had tricked me into believing she was some poor girl just like me, desperate to be included; or—this somehow felt like the worst possibility—grateful that her deception had prevented my total humiliation.

"Hey," Ellie said, "I was just trying to help out. You're not mad or anything, right?" Her droopy eyes were slightly watery again.

The truth was, I wanted to be friends with her. She was unpredictable, popular, Jake's sister. All very good things. But I still felt like I needed some loophole to act okay with what she had done. "Were you really just trying to help me?" I asked.

"Yeah," Ellie said, with zero hesitation. "Totally."

"Then no . . . I'm not mad."

Ellie smiled, her watery eyes suddenly dry. She lifted her hand, extending her pinky with a grand gesture. "So, friends?"

I let her finger slip into mine. And when she gave it a hard twist, the disco lights casting a shadow across our linked hands, I pushed all doubt aside and said, "Friends."

11.

Your Christmas card, the one
with that cheerful picture of
you with your family lounging
beneath a palm tree.

Did you notice how much your
little girl looks like me?

It's proof, don't you think?

That nothing between us is
sacred, not even the most
invisible lines.

Jake

AFTER. FEBRUARY.

Amber comes to my dorm room with her long hair in pigtails and boots on her feet. She doesn't say hello or wait to be invited in. She simply sways on by. When I turn around, she's leaning against my window, staring at me.

She says, "I haven't seen you in a while, kiddo. You never returned my texts, and Janie says you haven't been to lit class in weeks . . ."

I haven't seen Amber since Ellie died. But I do vaguely recall the texts and e-mails she sent in December, a drunk-dial voice mail on New Year's Eve, a Post-it note stuck on my door in January. "Who the fuck is Janie?" I ask.

"She's my roommate. She's in your class. Anyway . . ." Her

voice rises lightly, like she realizes we've gotten off to a bad start. "Seriously, though . . ." She sets her jacket on the window ledge and sighs. "Have you gone into hiding?"

She brings her eyes back to mine, but I can't hold her gaze, because all I can see is that night, that final phone call with Ellie, and suddenly it's hard to breathe.

"You okay?" she asks.

I stare at my feet. "I'm fine." I pull my hands away from my temple and the headache that's been there since I got back from Ohio.

"To be absolutely honest," she says, her gentle voice piercing, "I heard about your sister, and I thought maybe you needed someone to . . . you know . . . talk to about it."

I lift my eyes. She's still watching me, her head resting against the windowpane. "What's to talk about?" I ask dully.

"I don't know. When's the last time you went to class? Any class?" She pauses. "You look like hell. When's the last time you left this room?"

"Why is that your business?"

Her forehead wrinkles in surprise. She retreats a little then. Looks out the window at the street traffic below. It's an all-too-familiar view. For the last few months I've missed class after class, lost in the monotonous lives of those tiny people, the fascinating predictability of the traffic lights as they change from green to red.

Amber says, "I can see the bar we met at that one time. It's right . . ." She extends her index finger toward something beyond the pane, and her voice fades away. Her hand falls to her side. "Do you ever think about probabilities?"

"As in . . . ?" I reply, not quite sure where she's going with this or why she's even still here.

"As in what are the chances"—she clears her throat—"of being hit by lightning twice? Or two planes crashing in one week?" She laughs hollowly. "Sometimes, I console myself with probabilities. Like if a plane crashes the week I'm supposed to fly, I say, 'Well, thank God that's out of the way.'"

I don't know what she's talking about. Or why she's now striding across the room, stepping over piles of dirty clothes and forgotten bags of take-out food. I only know I'd rather stand at the edge alone than be here with her.

She stops beside a chair and stares down at a large cardboard box filled with letters, sketch pads, and pictures. She tilts the box toward her, her eyes raking the contents. "Ellie's things?" she whispers.

"Please, don't." Hearing her say Ellie's name is too much, and I feel that all-too-familiar pain in my chest. That pain that sometimes feels like it could tear me apart. "Just go. There's nothing you know about this."

There is a long silence, and then she is beside me, reaching for me. I take a step back and another and another until I am where she began. The cold glass presses against my skin. She's breaths away. "Jake . . ." She touches the side of my face, but I push her hand off. "What were the chances of us meeting that night, of me being here when she called? It seems so improbable. So unlikely, and ever since I found out, I keep thinking . . ." Her voice cracks. Her eyes fill with tears. "What were the chances?"

"What difference does it make?" I ask, but I know what she knows: I know it made all the difference in the world. And I finally understand the reason for her visit. Why she just gave me her little speech. She needs what we all need: forgiveness.

"Jake . . ." She strokes my chest. It feels strange to have another person's hand on me, to hear another person's voice beside me. "If we had never met . . ." Her eyes search mine. "If I had let you go . . ." She presses against me.

"Amber, *please*." I push against the window, but there's nowhere else to go. For months my head has pounded with all the *could have*s and *should have*s, Ellie's words constantly ringing in my ears: *If I need you, you'll come back for me?*

Amber's lips slide across my neck. She whispers, "I just need you to know how incredibly terrible I feel. . . . I'll never forgive myself." She lays her head on my chest, her guilt soaking my T-shirt, as she says over and over again, "I'm so sorry."

When she kisses me, I don't stop her. I let her lead me to the bed. I let her turn out the lights. And when she runs her hands down my back, I tell myself not to think about what comes next. That what we're doing is okay. That this is what I need to feel better—the darkness of this night. The illusion that love is near.

12.

I miss sixth grade and that
time you convinced me to
play Barbies in your bedroom.
We drew the shades tightly,
afraid that someone might use
a ladder to scale your walls
and find us there, still being
children.

Jessie

BEFORE. JULY.

We crouched in the bushes outside Tommy's bedroom. Lola heaved loudly, like we had just walked a mile instead of a hundred feet. She looked like she might cry, but as far as I knew, Lola hadn't cried all year.

"What's going on?" I finally asked.

She stared at the grass like she was counting the number of blades. A butterfly darted by, and I watched its wings flutter, a smear of yellow and black fighting hard against a sudden current of wind.

"Lola," I said gently, "can you at least tell me why we're here?"

She started to cry then, and I couldn't help but think that her cry was like some sort of a miracle, like seeing Jesus in a grilled cheese sandwich or something. Eventually, she wiped her hand across her nose, snot clinging to the edge of her wrist. She pushed her hair into her face and shook her head, like she wanted to keep whatever it was to herself. But then she said, "A few months ago I was leaving your house and Tommy was there and he asked if he could walk with me a bit . . ."

She took a deep breath before continuing, her voice nearly mechanical, as if she had gone over this story a hundred times in her head. "We were just walking and joking around about nothing, really, but then he grabbed my hand and said I was pretty."

The music stopped, leaving us with the light sound of Sarah's laughter. Lola cringed. When the music started up again, she continued, her voice harder than before. "My mom was out on a date with some new loser, and Tommy had some . . ." She halted; her expression made it clear she didn't want to tell me.

"What, Lola? What did he have?"

She cleared her throat. "Pot."

"But you didn't, right?" Lola had been the president of our sixth-grade D.A.R.E. chapter, and the first person to make fun of anyone holding a cigarette, but I knew that didn't mean a thing if a boy was factored into the equation.

"God, Jess"—her voice rose defensively—"I said no, okay? Give me some credit. But he wanted to go, and you know I can't stand being in that house alone, especially at night. It's just so spooky without my dad there and all those empty rooms. So I asked him to come in and *just* hang out."

"So you didn't smoke?" I asked. The guilt on her face was as good as any answer.

She wrapped her arms around her knees. "I just wanted to know if it was as fun as he said, but it didn't work. Okay? Tommy says I don't know how to inhale."

I rolled my eyes, and she looked away, shrugging. "It's not that big of a deal, really."

"Then why were you crying?" I asked.

She was quiet for a long while. "He just kept calling and coming over. And I thought he really liked me." She paused, and her eyes found mine. "He actually said it, you know? He said, 'I like you, Lola.'" Again she stopped talking. I could tell she was trying to pull herself together, but when she started up again, it was clear she was still sliding. "I wouldn't have done it, Jess. I swear, if I hadn't thought . . ." She started crying again, her tears picking up speed. I pulled her close, trying to muffle the sounds of it with my body.

"Hey, it's going to be okay," I said, but my sympathy only made her cry harder. After a while her sobbing subsided, but she continued to cling to me, her wet face pressed to my shirt.

In the silence, her words—and what they meant—hovered above us: big, important, irreversible.

Sex.

This was the biggest secret she had ever kept from me. Finally, I asked, "Are you and Tommy together now? Is that why you're so upset?"

She shook her head, and in a small voice said, "He barely even looks at me in the hallway."

I felt a pang inside me, imagining what it felt like to give away so much for so little. Without thinking, I kissed the top of her head and smoothed her hair. It was the only thing I knew to do. It's what I did to Mattie whenever she was upset, but Lola wasn't Mattie, and instead of curling into me, she pulled away.

She leaned her head back against the exterior wall and stared at the sky, tears silently seeping out of her eyes. I held out my hand, and, for once, she took it.

We didn't notice Ellie until she sat down beside us, looking like a fairy with her translucent skin, blue crinoline skirt, and sheer peasant top.

"Spying on Tommy and Sarah?" she said. Her pink lips turned up into a smirk.

Normally, Lola led in these kinds of situations, but she stayed silent, quickly hiding her wet face behind a curtain of hair. I was still trying to think of a response when Ellie glanced at me, her smirk flatlining, and said, "God, these mosquitoes are biting the shit out of me. Let's get out of here."

She crawled out from behind the cottage and headed toward the house. We followed. Inside, Ellie said to Lola, "Go wash your face. Come to my room"—she pointed at a half-open door—"when you're done."

I had never been inside Ellie's room, and when we crossed the threshold, I was surprised by its brightness. The walls were buttercup yellow, and stars the color of tangerines hung from the ceiling. Fireflies with watermelon-colored tails were painted in a zigzag pattern around the window, like they had swarmed in from outside. Taped to the desk behind me were dozens of Polaroids of Ellie and Sarah. One looked as recent as yesterday.

"So . . ." Ellie moved beside me, our shoulders touching as she leaned back against the desk. "Spying, huh?"

I was silent. I always had a hard time talking around Ellie. She made up for her small stature with an intimidating personality. After a while, she sighed and went to her dresser. She took out a pack of cigarettes and lit one with a bright blue lighter, the casing covered with a Hello Kitty sticker that looked like the kind Mattie had in her room.

"Smoke?" She held out the pack, but I shook my head. She tucked it into her back pocket. Then, after several puffs, tapped the ashes into a nearby cup and said, "So? You. Lola. Tommy's window . . ."

Again, I said nothing.

"You're fucking hilarious," she said. "You're like a mute version of Sarah."

Her eyes were rimmed with blacker-than-black eyeliner and midnight blue eye shadow. I wondered what she looked like without all that makeup. "It's okay." She flicked away more ashes. "You don't have to be embarrassed. Sometimes we all like to watch."

"I wasn't watching," I said. "And I don't look like Sarah, either." I squared my shoulders, trying to look tougher than I felt. In the bathroom, Lola coughed loudly.

"God," Ellie said. "Tommy's not worth all this drama."

"You know about that?" I asked, surprised.

She smiled and said, "You catch on quick."

"And Sarah? Does she know Tommy hooked up with Lola?" I wasn't sure if I really wanted to know the answer to this. My sister was self-centered, but I couldn't believe she'd knowingly hurt Lola. Still, people had a way of surprising you.

"Sarah'd be shocked by what she knew if she took the time to

CARMEN RODRIGUES

think about it. But for now, I think she's just happy being oblivious to all this." Ellie inched forward, filling the space between us with smoke. I coughed nervously, leaning back as far as I could.

"But why don't you just tell her?" I said to break the silence. "Aren't you supposed to be her best friend?"

"Why don't *you* tell her?" Ellie whispered, so close now the tips of our shoes touched. "Aren't *you* supposed to be her sister?" We stared at each other. Her hand moved so that I felt her fingers graze mine. "No, you don't look like Sarah." Her voice sounded bored, but she seemed almost nervous. "I've always thought you were prettier."

She moved away, sitting on the edge of her bed like nothing had happened. I slumped against the desk, my heart beating erratically. I glanced at Ellie. She was still watching me.

"What?" She smiled that weird smile of hers, half nice but also half mean.

"Nothing," I said.

Lola walked in. She seemed more composed. Her hair was pulled into a neat ponytail, her eyes red but dry. "Thanks," she said to Ellie.

"Don't worry about it." Ellie pulled the pack of cigarettes from her back pocket, flipped the cardboard lid open, and extended it to Lola, who promptly took one.

"Doesn't your mom care if you smoke in the house?" I glanced at Lola.

"My mom couldn't care less. Plus, she's working." Ellie lit Lola's cigarette and laughed. "Don't be such a priss-bitch, *Jess.* Nobody likes a priss-bitch."

The words stung, but I tried to conceal my hurt. I looked down at my half-painted toenails and hoped the flush spreading across my face might fade quickly.

"She's so stupid about things like this," Lola said, coughing.

"Yeah? Like how?" Ellie sounded genuinely interested, which shocked me. Most of the time she treated me the way Lola treated Meg.

"Lola," I warned, knowing she would bring up the party. It was all I had heard about for the last week. "Don't—"

"Jessie." Lola gave me a look that said *Shut up* and continued without pause. "So, at Todd Michael's party last week, she"— Lola waved her cigarette in my direction—"wouldn't go 'cause his parents weren't home."

"That's not true," I said. "I just didn't want to go."

"She's lying," Lola said. "She didn't go 'cause his parents weren't home, and she's afraid a boy will try and kiss her if there aren't any parents around. Like that would be the worst thing in the world. Like, hello? I got my first kiss in sixth grade, and Jess is freakin' fifteen and never been kissed. Lame, right? I mean—"

Lola continued to speak, but I tuned her out, my cheeks burning red. I already felt like an idiot where Ellie was concerned, and now . . .

"Is that true, Jess?" Ellie asked.

"It's so true!" Lola said. "She's so—"

"Is your name Jess?" Ellie said dryly. "Well, *Jess*, is it?"

I glanced at her curious face, every part of my body tingling with embarrassment. I nodded, and her expression changed, almost seeming sympathetic.

The room was quiet, except for Lola, who coughed nervously.

I stared down at my toes again, waiting for what would come next—some kind of joint taunting—and was surprised when Ellie said, "*Well* . . . we can change that right now."

Lola laughed. *"How?"*

"I'll kiss her," Ellie said simply.

"Wh-what?" she said.

"What?" I echoed, snapping my head up. Ellie was walking toward me. The closer she got, the hotter I felt. It was nearly unbearable.

"But that's fucking gay," Lola said, and I nodded automatically.

"What are you, a homophobe, Lola?" Ellie was next to me

now. "Besides, I'm kissing Jess so she knows what it's like. It's more like practicing." She arched an eyebrow at Lola. "Right?"

"I—I don't think so," Lola stammered.

"Well . . . ," Ellie said. "Look at it this way: I'm helping Jess out by teaching her how to kiss. That's, like, for a good cause. But *you* slept with Tommy because you wanted him to like you. And that's just sad and pathetic. So, which is worse?"

Lola was quiet. Her cigarette dangled halfway from her mouth. Even though she had it coming, I still felt bad for her. Ellie in mean-girl mode was a scary thing. I couldn't count the number of times I'd watched her reduce the school's most confident, popular girls to tears without a blink of her lifeless blue eyes.

"I don't know where you heard that, but that's not true," Lola said, her voice rising. "Okay? It's a lie. And I don't appreciate you telling lies about me."

Ellie rolled her eyes. "Tommy's telling everyone otherwise."

"No, he's not," Lola insisted, her eyes glassy.

"What did you expect?" Ellie asked calmly. "That he thought you were special? That you were together?"

Lola put out her cigarette in the cup. She turned toward the window and took her hair out of the ponytail.

"Oh, God," Ellie said in her usual bored way. "She's crying again."

Lola shook her head. After a while she said, "I'm done with Tommy, okay?"

Ellie laughed, crossed to Lola, and placed her hands on her shoulders. She glanced at me and winked, like this was our inside joke, but I didn't understand what any of it had to do with me. "Lola, you can't be so sensitive. I mean, you were a total bitch to Jess just now, but you don't see her crying. And you know why? 'Cause Jess is tough and you're a wimp."

And then I understood. In her own twisted way, Ellie was defending me.

"Okay?" Ellie said, and I saw her grip on Lola's shoulders tighten.

"Yeah, whatever," Lola said, and Ellie let her go.

"Maybe you should go home," she said.

Lola nodded slowly, but didn't move.

"Go on," Ellie repeated.

"Jess?" It was just like before, only this time it wasn't Meg giving me the pleading look; it was Lola. I wanted to feel sorry for her, but I couldn't.

"Jess is staying," Ellie said. Her words set off some sort of sensation inside me that I couldn't identify. I just knew I wanted to stay as much as I wanted to go.

"Right," Lola said, still frozen. Finally, she dragged her feet across the floor. A minute later, the front door slammed shut.

I looked up, and Ellie smiled. "I don't know why you put up with her. She's such a bitch."

"She's not always like that," I said. Ellie gave me a doubtful look, so I added, "Her parents just got divorced."

"So, what's that got to do with anything?" Ellie said. "My mom's on her third marriage."

If anything, Ellie was proving my point, but I knew better than to say as much. We were quiet then, and Ellie picked a Polaroid off her desk and stared at it absently, flicking the edge of the photograph with her finger. She seemed jittery. "Are you mad at me?" she asked.

I shrugged my shoulders, feeling torn. Nobody had ever stood up for me like that, and Lola did kind of deserve it, but still . . . "I don't know what to think. Maybe I should go," I said.

Ellie set the Polaroid aside. She moved closer until, once again, our fingers touched.

"Ellie, please . . ." There was that sensation again. It felt almost like a jolt of electricity.

"She had it coming. You can't always be so nice, Jess," she said.

"You can't always be so mean," I replied, without thinking. It was the most honest thing I had ever said to her.

She smiled, nearly appreciative. "See," she said, "that's better. You weren't nice, but you were fair." She set her palm against my cheek, and my chin began to quiver. I was filled with both an irrational desire to press my lips to her palm, and a fear that I wouldn't be able to control this strange impulse. I tried to stop the shaking by making my body rigid. I locked my knees and stiffened my arms, but nothing worked. I debated fleeing when Ellie pressed forward, her lips drifting lightly across mine.

She leaned back to gauge my reaction. "Is that okay?" Her hand was suddenly on my waist, sliding up my abdomen until her fingers rested tentatively below my breasts.

I didn't think very much before I nodded.

"Good." She smiled. Then, once again, she pressed her mouth to mine. This time her lips were firmer, her tongue soft and wet. I closed my eyes, and even though I knew it was wrong, I let her kiss me for a long time.

13.

You're the opposite of known.

Sarah
AFTER. FEBRUARY.

"So, are you ready to begin?" Concerned Therapist taps her pen against her temple and releases a sigh that rustles her plump lips. She seems tired today. A headband pulls hair away from her face. Her eyes are puffy. Her mascara is slightly smeared.

It's another Wednesday, another session, and I'm watching her, wondering how long she can keep up this *I'm really interested in your life* charade. I bet it's not for long. The sigh is just the first crack in our relationship. Soon there will be more sighs, or Concerned Therapist will begin to watch the clock. Or she'll forget to set her cell phone to vibrate, or she'll hide her yawn behind the fabric of her sweater. Things will fall apart, just not today. Today, Concerned Therapist decides to sit up straight and stare at me in an appropriate Concerned Therapist way. She says again, in a clearer voice, "Are you ready to begin?"

The truth is, I'm not ready to begin, but in here that doesn't really matter. Three months of therapy have taught me that nobody is interested in that type of honesty. So I settle into the worn leather sofa, pull a silver pillow onto my lap, and say, "Yeah, I'm ready."

"I talked to your mom for a bit yesterday." Concerned Therapist tucks the pen behind her ear and absently rubs the corner of her eye with her right index finger. "She mentioned you and Ellie were part of a foursome." She looks at her notes. "You, Ellie, Tommy, and Jake. Do you want to tell me a little bit about them? About the things you guys used to do together?"

And here it is: the loaded question.

"You do know," Concerned Therapist says to my silence, "that everything you say in this room is confidential." Her finger remains near the corner of her eye, as if she anticipates it will need attention soon. This is an opportunity to push the conversation in a new direction.

"Are you tired?" I ask.

"No, not really," she says.

"You look tired." I lean forward, press my elbows into my knees, and give her the empathetic look. "You've got, you know"—I point to the area beneath my eyes—"bags."

"Do I?" She moves her finger away, like I've made her feel self-conscious. This small victory makes me happy.

"Sarah, tell me about . . ." Again, she looks down at her notes. "Jake."

I wonder if she's picked this name at random or if this is Concerned Therapist's second trick of the day: the ace up her sleeve. I pull the pillow closer to my body. It smells like Old Spice or something else my grandfather would wear. I wonder if this Old Spice man came to Concerned Therapist to discuss a dead wife, estranged children, or erectile dysfunction. I wonder if he came willingly because he had this aching desire to understand a history he'd bottled up inside. Maybe he did, or maybe he was forced into it by his family.

"Jake is Ellie's older brother. That's it," I tell her.

"That's it. *Really?*" The therapist crosses her legs and leans forward. Her skirt rides up, and I see the blackish tentacles of a spider vein spreading along the inside of her left knee. I wonder if she knows the vein is there, if it embarrasses her.

"Sarah, your mother seems to think you and Jake were close. Why would she tell me that?" This statement surprises me. It indicates my mom has a clue about my life, which I'm pretty sure she does not . . .

Or does she? I shift farther into my seat, wondering what my mom does and doesn't know. Then I finally say, "I don't know." It's plain and simple and the truth. Besides, even if I wanted to talk to her about Jake, which I don't, I couldn't begin to explain what we were. We weren't friends, enemies, or lovers. We were something undefined. "He's Ellie's brother, that's all."

"That's all?" she repeats. This is a typical Concerned Therapist tactic, like repetition helps elicit some sort of deeper response. "Jake was your best friend's brother. You must have spent a lot of time with him, too. You must have learned something about him."

"I guess," I say vaguely, and then I make a face like this is a new thought to me and I'm giving it my utmost consideration. "Let me think about it . . ."

Often, to pass the time with Concerned Therapist, I share a variety of insignificant details about my life. I deliver these facts in an overly dramatic fashion, so she believes they carry a lot of weight. That's what I'm about to do now. After I've given it some *serious* thought, I sigh loudly, and say, "Jake's eyes are nearly indigo, sometimes black."

"Go on." She jots something in her notebook. I bet it says *Opening up. Good job!*

I say with another big sigh, "Jake has a brown freckle in his left eye, just shy of his iris."

"Uh-huh." Concerned Therapist writes something else down. I bet it says *Interesting!* Then she looks back at me, waiting for me to continue, but I simply shrug and shut up. And here her face shifts from hope to disappointment. As it does, I think about that brown freckle in Jake's eye, how I used to wonder about it sometimes, and it is this random, insignificant thought that creates the tiniest wormhole for the past to slide into the present.

"What are you thinking right now?" Concerned Therapist scoots closer, like she senses there are real secrets waiting. Her voice is firm. "Tell me. Tell me what you're thinking right now."

"I'm not thinking anything," I say, but I'm thinking about Jake and Ellie, and everything in between. My mind is suddenly spinning back and forth until it settles on one distinct memory: a year ago, the time when Ellie's parents were both out of town and I spent the night at her house. We thought we'd be alone for the whole weekend. Then her stepfather returned early from a business trip.

"Sarah?" Concerned Therapist moves to the edge of her seat. "Is there something you want to tell me?"

Again, I shift in my seat. I look just past her, out the window at the traffic rushing by, the people-filled cars that magically disappear from sight. "Nope. Not a thing."

"Are you sure?" She glances at the clock. But I am silent. I am silent until finally she sighs and says, "Well, I guess we're just about out of time." She jots down a few more notes, grabs her desk calendar, and heads to the waiting room to discuss next week's appointment with my mom.

I linger behind, continuing to watch the cars. I imagine myself inside one, hurtling blissfully into the great beyond.

BEFORE. MARCH.

We stood in the living room. Me with alcohol coating my lips, and Ellie's stepdad with his carry-on suitcase teetering beside him. He had entered the house a minute earlier, and when he saw me standing near the liquor cabinet, he asked, "Where's Ellie?" Then his eyes lowered to my skimpy nightshirt—the one I had worn specifically to catch Jake's attention—and his face registered a familiar look of disappointment.

"*Um . . .*" I moved closer to the wall, curling my shoulders inward. I was still completely buzzed from earlier, when Ellie had convinced me to dress up like a *Mad Men* character—our hair in French twists, Jackie O sunglasses on our faces—and drink martini after martini while we danced to some Motown records her real dad had left behind.

"Oh, hey, Sargeant." Ellie was beside me, dressed in a slinky red nightgown that belonged to her mother. She walked toward him, outstretched arms pulling him close like a long-lost lover. "You're back early," she said, her eyes glazed.

He stepped away, obviously uncomfortable. He glanced at the living room, running his stubby fingers through thin brown hair. Wrinkles washed over his forehead, creasing the sides of his cheeks. His eyes hesitated at the dirty dishes on a side table and traveled to an empty martini glass atop the open liquor cabinet.

"Come on, Ellie." Weariness crept into his voice. "You're almost seventeen now. It's time to stop all this nonsense."

Ellie brushed her bangs from her face and rubbed her hand across the space beneath her lips, her eyelids at half-mast, her voice seductive. "I'm just curious. Haven't you ever been curious?"

"Ellie . . ." He shook his head and sighed, all the while repeating her name. "Ellie. Ellie, listen to me. I can't keep going around in circles like this with you. I told you, if you keep on like this, I'm going to have to talk to your mom." He held up his hands, and his face looked pained. "You're not giving me any choices here—"

"You don't need to tell her anything." Her eyes narrowed. "Besides, there's nothing to tell. Yet . . ." She trailed her hand down his chest, her finger tracing the buttons of his work shirt from his collar to his belt buckle.

"Stop! Okay? Just stop! I'm tired of this." He shoved her away, and she stumbled backward, landing in a big heap on the sofa. She began to laugh, a loud cackling sound that made my skin crawl.

Suddenly, the room began to spin; the air seemed nearly sucked out of it. I pressed my palm to the wall, using it to steady me as I made my way toward Ellie's bedroom. Inside, I slipped her window open and pushed my face against the screen. The night air was frigid, but I let it swirl around me until the coldness became unbearable. Then I started to gather my things while Ellie's words, like intrusive thoughts, rammed against me: *Haven't you ever been curious? Haven't you ever been curious? Haven't you ever been curious?*

I stopped to rest my head against the windowsill—waiting, breathing—but my anxiety continued to grow. Ellie entered the room five minutes later and halted beside my overnight bag. "What? Are you leaving?"

I gazed at her blurry figure. I wanted to ask her what she was doing. Why she always got like this. But I knew how that conversation would go, and I just couldn't take a big scene, not right then. "I don't feel well."

"You don't feel well?" Ellie repeated slowly. "You were fine, like, five minutes ago. Is it Sargeant?" She always called him by his last name, never his first, which was Gary. "Oh, come on. You know what a sucker he is. Please." She took a sip from yet another martini glass. "I just don't get what your deal is."

"What are you doing?" I stood, my hand on the bedpost, and turned to face her.

She thrust her drink forward, and gin spilled onto the floor. "I'm drinking. I . . ." She tried to laugh, but the sound caught in her throat. "I don't understand." Again, she smiled. "Are you really sick?" The vacancy in her eyes started to be replaced with some form of comprehension, maybe even concern.

I watched the glass, the way the clear liquid swayed. There was so much I wanted to say, but all I could do was move my fingers across my lips as if I might communicate through sign language.

"I don't understand," Ellie repeated.

"It's like you're two different people sometimes," I said, and grabbed my bag.

"What are you talking about?" She held on to my wrist, but

I squirmed free. I didn't stop when she called my name, her footsteps chasing me through the hallway, or when I heard her say, "Sarah, you're making a big deal out of nothing. I don't even know what you're talking about. Nothing happened!" I kept moving, until the kitchen's sliding glass doors shut firmly behind me, my body filled with a sudden sense of safety.

At the edge of the pool, I stopped to breathe. I gripped a tree, the bark scratching my skin. When I turned back, I saw Ellie through her kitchen window, standing over the sink, her eyes filled with confusion. I wanted to go back and say it would be all right, but I didn't believe that anymore. Tears streamed down my face as the emotions settled across hers. And just for a minute, she seemed like that same little girl I met when we were twelve. But seconds later, she raised her drink, and I saw the grown-up Ellie, the one I secretly wanted to leave behind.

14.

Some days I want to tell you
that I can't do it on my own.
But even on those days, I
can't bring myself to say these
things to someone who might not
always be here.

Jake
AFTER. FEBRUARY.

When we're done, Amber pulls a half-full bottle of wine from her bag and says, "I had a rough childhood, you know." She rubs my back, telling me every horrible story she can muster: bad baby-sitters, a dickhead dad who worked too much, an uncle who once popped her on the mouth for saying "shit."

Hours later the bottle's empty, and Amber, bleary-eyed, puts on her silvery boots, says "Fuck! The time!" and disappears.

After she's gone, I spin her empty bottle and stare at Ellie's box. For months now I've imagined myself going through the contents: sorting her letters, pictures, and sketch pads into evidence of who Ellie was, who she wanted to be, the things I never knew about her, the things I knew but didn't want to see. I can only take so much of these thoughts before that pain that I get sometimes overwhelms me, and then I'm grateful for any distraction, like when my cell phone rings.

"I just wanted to hear your voice," Mom says when I answer. She sounds breathless. It's how she talks these days. Sentences filled with urgency and air but also, conflictingly, hesitation and the threat of tears.

I sit on the edge of the bed, automatically falling into my routine performance of a caring son. I ask her how she is, and she responds positively. Then we chat about the fine Arizona weather, and that leads to yet another request for me to visit her. "You'll see, the state is lovely," she says, enduring my awkward silence before finally arriving at another story, another apology, another "aha moment" unearthed from the bowels of group therapy.

This is what residents of Full Circle Spa do. They practice warrior poses, seek enlightenment through meditative trances, pat a neighbor's hand consolingly during group time, and reach out to their families for understanding. And we answer because we feel terrible if we don't.

She begins her "aha moment." As usual, I tune in and out, only catching fragments of this latest revelation: "I never really thought about how having an alcoholic father affected me. You

know, I just kept telling myself he had a temper and a rough job, and he was functional, so it was hard to think that he was just like other people's drunk dads . . ."

We talk about her dad a lot lately. How he used to hit her when he was drunk, how he used to belittle her if she did poorly in school, how her brothers had it worse because her dad would *raise only strong men*. This image of my mom, helpless against her dad's tirades, only increases my pain. So I tune out for an even greater period of time, still managing to fill the gaps between her sentences with "yes" and "okay" and "I see."

When I tune back in, she's saying, "I loved finding you there, but I never told you that. I'm sorry that I didn't, Jake. You kept reading all those books by Mark Twain. Remember?"

Apparently, we've fast-forwarded past her childhood and into mine. She's talking about the summer I was ten. I used to stay up long after Ellie fell asleep and wait for her to come home from work.

She launches into her remembrance of those tender late-night reunions. I also privately return to that time. For the most part my recollection is hazy, but I remember what I can: her grilled-cheese sandwiches with a side of chips; sitting at the edge of the pool, feet submerged in cold water, warm plates against our thighs; her wine spilling onto the grout between the

pavers. How I lied to make her feel better about her twelve-hour shifts, saying Ms. Sullivan made *terrible* dinners, even though Ms. Sullivan made *excellent* dinners. How, always, Mom's cigarettes and wine wore the night away, leading us to the moment when she'd turn to me with glassy eyes and deliver a rant about my father.

This is a part I remember clearly: "Responsible men don't run off to Florida with a coworker. Responsible men don't leave a wife and children behind. Responsible men don't break their vows. Jake—" She'd always freeze here, like a swimmer on a platform reconsidering a ten-meter dive. "Jake, promise me you'll always be responsible. That you'll never break your word. That you'll never be like *him*."

She'd put her hand over mine then, and nothing would loosen her grip but my pledge that I'd be *different* and *better*. I gave this pledge over and over again, until she slackened her hold, murmuring something like, "You love us. You love Ellie. You'll never leave us."

But I had left with false promises and reassurances, proving I was *no different* or *better* than my father.

Mom stops rambling. She asks, "Were those times just as special for you?"

The response is automatic. "Yes, Mom."

"Good. Good." The phone beeps, and she sighs apologetically. "I have to go now. Think about what I said, okay? It's nice and warm here. A perfect weekend getaway."

"Yeah, sure." My voice is flattened by disinterest, and I hear the hurt in her good-bye.

Alone again, I slide down to the floor and rest my head on the mattress. I reach for Amber's empty bottle until I feel it pressed against my skin: solid, cold, painfully empty of hope.

15.

That Hello Kitty sticker reminds
me of being eleven, of being
okay, of a time when my mind
had less racing thoughts. You
remind me of these things too.

Jessie
BEFORE. AUGUST.

Lola changed into her gray pajamas, pulling the bottoms up so quickly the elastic band snapped around the waist. "That's bullshit," she said, glancing at my backpack, which lay innocently in the corner of my bedroom. "You had to have found something. I mean, you searched her entire room, right?"

It was a Friday night, and until a few hours earlier, I had sat on my bed, tearing through the last novel on my summer reading list. To be honest, it was an act of desperation. For the past month, all I could think about was Ellie and our kiss. And the only thing that seemed to get my mind off it was reading. It was like my mom said: *Sometimes, the only way to get off one distraction is get on another. Just pick something that might do you a bit more good.*

So far, all that my thinking about Ellie had done was create a lot of anxiety. At least with the reading, I'd be ahead in school. I was just about to reach the climax of the novel when Lola showed up. She was dressed entirely in black, her long brown hair twisted up into a tight bun. This was not her usual look. Lola preferred short skirts and loose curls.

"What's up with the outfit? Aren't you supposed to be at your dad's?"

"He forgot. Again." She sat on the edge of my bed and unloaded her overnight bag, which had two walkie-talkies, a flashlight, and a pair of binoculars. Then she explained her plan.

Afterward, she looked at me, her eyes intense, and said, "So, are you in or out?"

I stared at her blankly. I couldn't tell if she was serious about breaking into Ellie's house. But if she was, she had it all figured out. Somehow she knew that Ellie's parents had left that afternoon to attend a medical conference in Baltimore. *Your sister mentioned it at dinner two nights ago.* That Tommy, Sarah, and Ellie would be at the movies. *Again, at dinner.* That the spare key to Ellie's house was hidden beneath a faux frog in their yard. *Remember? I saw Jake use it that one time he got locked out.*

"I just need you to stand guard, and I'll do the rest," she said.

From what I gathered, "do the rest" meant her searching Ellie's room for something that could potentially destroy her—a diary, incriminating photo, or medical proof she had some sort of STD.

"Have you been watching *Gossip Girl* again?" I asked.

"Very funny." Her eyes narrowed. "She's a bitch. And you want to know what? I asked Tommy today about what she said, and he said it wasn't true. Not any of it."

I watched a bit of pain shoot across her face. "Tommy's a liar," I said. "Besides, how would Ellie know about any of it if he hadn't told her?"

She shrugged, unconcerned with the details, as if Tommy's word was enough. "Maybe she was spying?"

"On you and Tommy?" I asked incredulously. She had really gone off the deep end if she even believed that was possible.

"We were spying on Tommy and Sarah. What's the difference?" she said, as if this proved her point. "So are you going to help me or not?"

She was determined, and I knew that with or without me, she was going in. There was no time to warn Ellie, and the only other option was to tell my mom, but I couldn't imagine ratting Lola out that way. I searched my mind for other possibilities and came up with only one.

"I'll help you," I said, "but only if I go in *alone*."

She opened her mouth to protest, but I held up a hand to

silence her. "Just wait. Okay? I know the house better than you do. I'll be faster and have less of a chance of getting caught."

I didn't add that I wanted to go in. That the idea excited me more than I'd care to admit.

She considered this for a while, but still seemed reluctant.

"It's the only way I'll help you," I said.

Twenty minutes later I stood inside Ellie's room, flashlight in hand. It was weird standing there, dressed in Lola's black leotard and leggings, running my hands freely across Ellie's desk. I felt a series of conflicting emotions: guilty and happy, brave and cowardly. Mostly, I felt changed.

Until a month ago, I had never kissed anyone, I had never lied to Lola, and I had never broken the rules. Not like this. And now here I was, standing in Ellie's bedroom, cataloging her life.

I stared at some of the photographs she had taped to the wall. Pictures of her with Jake, both smaller than the huge pumpkin behind them; with Sarah at her sweet-sixteen party; and with her dad, when she was about seven.

I picked up that photo and stared at it more closely. I had never seen her look so animated. I flipped it over. On the back, scrawled in masculine handwriting, was *Me and my little Lee-Lee*. I had never met her father, but I knew on rare occasions Ellie disappeared to Florida for long-weekend visits with his new family.

"What's going on in there, Black Hawk?" Lola's voice burst through my receiver, calling me by the stupid code name she insisted on using.

"Nothing." I put the photo back and shifted my attention to the closet.

"Did you find anything?"

"Not yet."

"Well, hurry up."

"Okay," I muttered, already lost in Ellie's clothes—the soft fabrics, her favorite blue sweater. I found a scarf I'd seen her wear several times but not often enough to note its disappearance and slipped it into my backpack.

Then I stepped away from the closet, my foot connecting with something near her bed. I glanced down and saw them— a heap of black spiral notebooks now scattered on the floor. I sat eagerly on my heels and aimed my flashlight at notebook after notebook. They were all the same: dozens of sketches in charcoal, ink, and pencil. One, marked 2009, was of the creepy house on the corner, its telltale overgrown yard filling the page. Another was of the weird kid four houses over, the one with the big head and too-small eyes. One notebook had a series featuring Mr. Lumpnick's dog as he transitioned from puppy to adult.

I went to grab the next one in the stack, but it skidded beneath the bed. I flipped up the bed skirt and aimed my flashlight into the darkness: The notebook rested against an old shoe box that was about as far beneath Ellie's bed as you could get. It took a few tries, but finally with the tips of my fingers I was able to pull it out. The shoe box—somehow caught on the slightly bent edge of the spiral—came with it. I unlatched the two and then, mostly out of curiosity, slid the lid off the box.

"Black Hawk, car lights approaching the end of the block. Over."

Paper. Dozens of strips of paper torn haphazardly from a variety of sources, each with a cryptic message addressed to no one specific.

"Did you hear me, over?"

I rifled through the box, hands shaking. Was everything I wanted to know about Ellie here for the taking?

"The car is parking *now*. Are you *effing* deaf? Over."

I debated stealing the box and spending the entire night in the basement, reading each strip, trying to figure out its meaning.

"Getting *out* of the car. What the fuck are you doing?"

But if I stole the thing she held most private, would she ever forgive me?

"Jessie? Are you sh-shitting me? Are you n-nuts?" Lola was stuttering now. *"They're a-at the door!"*

I shoved the box under the bed and arranged the sketch pads—except for the one with this year's date—in a neat stack. That one I tossed into my bag, telling myself that I would find a way to return it in the morning, before Ellie noticed, and that it wasn't the same thing as taking her box. It was more like the scarf. It was only drawings, after all. But I knew I was lying to myself.

I raised Ellie's bedroom window just as the front door squeaked ajar. A woman's shaky voice said, "Well, we can just catch an early flight tomorrow. It's not a big deal, Gary. We should have just never stopped at the bar, okay? Can we just drop it now, okay?"

"Fine. I was just saying—" a deeper voice responded.

"I heard you the first, second, fourth, fifth—"

"Fine, consider it dropped," he snapped. They were silent then. I worked quietly at removing Ellie's screen—the latch on the left was rusted shut—while monitoring their noises. Luggage was dragged in, lamps turned on, and water run in the kitchen.

"Did you hear that?" Mr. Sargeant's voice cut the silence.

I froze, the pounding in my heart rising into my neck.

"Hear what?"

"Exactly. Where's Ellie? I thought she was grounded."

"She's sleeping over Sarah's house. Don't you remember I

told you? I'm sure I told you." Mrs. Sargeant's voice grew louder, coming to a halt right outside the door.

"She's never going to learn if you keep letting her out of her groundings," Mr. Sargeant said.

"I told you, we settled it. Why won't you let this go?"

"Because I don't believe her. And I'm tired of you taking her word over mine. If you honestly believe she's respecting your rules, there should be nothing in her room that says otherwise. So let's just end this argument by taking a look inside. . . ."

The door cracked open—the light from the hallway flooding the room—then, just as suddenly, slammed shut.

"Absolutely not! Gary, I'm not spy—"

"*Spying?* If you don't start paying more attention—"

"I'm exhausted. Do we have to discuss this now?" Her voice grew distant again. There was the click of another door, and then their sounds were completely muffled.

"*Psst*, Jess." I turned around. Lola stood outside Ellie's window, screen in hand.

Thirty minutes later, she was wearing her pajamas and interrogating me. "I just don't get it," she said.

"I told you, unless you want to tape up a charcoal drawing of Mr. Lumpnick's dog on everyone's locker, there was nothing there."

The sound of collective laughter drifted up from the living room, where my younger sisters were curled up with my parents on the couch, watching *The NeverEnding Story*. Just last summer I had spent most of my Friday nights right beside them, but high school had changed all that, making everything way more complicated.

"You looked underneath her bed? In her closet?"

"I'm sorry," I replied hollowly.

"Sorry?" Lola glared at me.

"Just relax. Okay? It was a dumb plan anyway."

"I knew I should have done it myself," she snapped.

"Yeah? In the dark? You hate being alone in the dark." I held her stare for a few minutes, and she looked away.

"What's gotten into you?" she asked suspiciously.

I shrugged, knowing that we were no longer talking about the break-in, but about my increasing ability to stand up to her.

"You're *hiding* something . . . aren't you?" She moved toward my backpack, but I jumped off my bed and blocked her. She gave me her typical *I'm going to tear your head off* look, but I held my ground. I didn't want her ripping through my things, tossing them and me around the way she did Mr. Big Butt Bear.

"I'm not lying."

"Then let me look." She took a step forward, her arms out

like a running back's. She tried to push past me, but much to her surprise and my own, I pushed back.

"Stop." I was shaking, filled with adrenaline.

"Move."

"No."

She grabbed my shoulders. I locked my legs and for a while was able to hold her, until she threw her height and weight into her lunge, forcing me aside. Within seconds she was dumping the contents of my bag onto the floor. She found the flashlight, Ellie's spare key, and the scarf, but not the sketch pad.

That I had somehow managed to drop in the bushes outside the kitchen door.

"You lied. You took a scarf," she hissed.

I straightened up. "I liked it."

We stared at each other.

"Fine. You know what? I'm going home. You're pathetic." She gathered her belongings, and a few of mine, like the snow globe she'd brought me back from Canada and the sequined headband she'd given me last Christmas. She paused beside a framed photo of us on my thirteenth birthday before tossing it in the trash can next to my dresser. Then she flicked off the lights and stormed out of my room, slamming the door shut.

I turned the lights back on and sat on my bed, waiting for

CARMEN RODRIGUES

my heart to calm. It didn't exactly return to normal—I felt too alive for that—but eventually, I stopped feeling so jumpy.

I knew that in a few days Lola would get over our fight. That's how it was with her. Little blowups that blew over eventually. But Ellie . . . what would she do if she found out about the sketch pad or the scarf? Just the thought alone made my heart clutch up.

Feeling like this was like standing on the edge of this cliff: I wanted to jump, even if the water turned out to be shallow.

I was tired of playing it safe. I wanted the free fall. And that scared me.

16.

You're only a year older than
me, but you've always been
so much wiser to the way this
world works. How everything
we've accumulated . . . mud on
my thigh, or a dandelion clinging
to the back of my wrist . . .
can be washed away.

Sarah
AFTER. FEBRUARY.

Another Sunday and my sisters go to church. I imagine them folded into pews, hymnbooks pressed against their thighs as they sing songs, hold hands, recite the Lord's Prayer.

I am home alone, with a soggy bowl of Cheerios in my lap, awaiting their return. And when they return, I watch them, trying to decipher their native rituals. I've learned many things about Sundays. But mostly I've learned that Mom sees and knows nearly everything, even if she pretends she does not.

She clears her throat when Meg mentions that Dad isn't home this Sunday like he promised. Sighs resolutely when Jess pretends to eat her food before pushing it aside. Smiles patiently as Mattie struggles to read a Dora the Explorer book.

When Meg, still in her Sunday best, races suddenly toward our living-room window, Mom chides her for her dangling barrettes and impossibly slippery hair. Meg ignores Mom and draws the plaid curtains aside, knocking a silver picture frame onto the carpet. She squeals, "He saw me! Oh my God!" Her cheeks turn pink, but she brazenly presses her body to the windowsill. "Oh, wait." She slowly exhales, staring at the nameless boy who is her latest fascination. "Wait."

Tires squeal. Meg dissolves into laughter. Mattie hops off Mom's lap, wanders to the window, and peeks outside. Jess pushes away her plate and joins the others to silently view the world beyond. Through the window, I can see that this day is glorious. Later it might turn cold and damp, but for right now the sun shines brightly and there is the promise of spring in the way the light wraps around the tree's bark. For the first time in months, I want to go outside, feel that sunshine on my face.

I move closer, but not too close, stopping to retrieve the picture frame. I stare at the happy family—a much glossier version of the one I know. When I set it back on the table, Mom catches my eye and nods toward the girls. "To be young," she says with a wistful smile, as if I am someone who has waged her own war with adulthood.

Now the room is absolutely muted—just the girls at the window and me staring at Mom.

Minutes pass, and the sounds begin to filter back in: Meg whispering to Jessie, and Mattie giggling.

Eventually, I go, "Mom . . ." And her head twitches in that mom way that means she'll respond if my voice rises in panic; otherwise, the dimmer is on and she's lost in her private thoughts. Still, the words continue forming slowly, first inside and then out: "Do you want to go for a walk—"

But my words are drowned out by Meg's booming voice. "Oh my God! Oh my God! I love him! I do!" She spins on her heels; her dangling barrette drops defiantly to the floor. She pretends to faint onto the couch, her legs comically straight in the air. Mattie, sensing the opportunity to play, takes a running leap and lands with a thud on Meg's body. Jess continues to stare out the window. Mom turns to me, her face preoccupied.

"Did you need something, Sarah?" she asks.

And it's this word "need"—the act of taking from her, not giving to or sharing with—that makes the sentence fold into some dark corner inside my body. I shake my head. She smiles kindly, the mom mask firmly in place.

On the couch, Meg tickles Mattie until she giggles uncontrollably.

And like that, the moment disappears.

That evening, I'm curled up in bed, watching Lifetime, when Tommy enters my room without knocking. I haven't seen him since our incident three weeks ago. Not one word in twenty-one days, but suddenly, as if by magic, he's back. And from the looks of it, all he wants is to examine my belongings.

He pauses beside my dresser, fingers the trinkets Mom's placed there to make this room feel more like my own: my grandparents' wedding picture, a tiny marble jewelry box she gave me when I turned seven, a hand-carved jade elephant my father brought back from a trip abroad. His hand stops when it reaches an unopened package. He runs his palm over the box's hard brown edges. Looks at the label. *Jake.* Then looks at me.

He's too far to touch—the edges of the area rug are barely beneath his Adidas—but I see his hand drift toward his mouth, the skin around his fingernails as raw today as three weeks before.

"Have you heard from him recently?" I ask.

He picks up the package, gives it a little shake. With it lying flat on his palm, he appears to estimate its weight. "Yeah," he says, "but he wasn't really making any sense. I think this whole thing with Ellie has him torn up." He sets the package back down. "When did this come?" he asks, too casually.

"I don't know. Last week, I think." I don't add that it's been sitting on my dresser ever since. That the thought of what's inside fills me with dread.

"Why haven't you opened it?" He taps the box. "Aren't you curious?"

I'm painfully curious. But I've also examined the evidence— Ellie's death, Jake's absence even before the hospital, the fact that nothing good has existed or ever will exist between us—and drawn the conclusion that what's in that box is another big fat piece of hell.

"Well?" Tommy prods.

I roll my eyes, poker faced, but there's something about the way Tommy looks at me, like he doesn't believe my bravado, that makes the other words tumble out. "Did he tell you he's never called? Not once since he left. He never even came to the hospital. He . . ." I continue on and on, fully aware that I sound like some whiny five-year-old chasing after an ice-cream truck. When I'm done, I wait for the inevitable: Tommy cracking a joke about how I must have my period or something. But he doesn't. He just sits on the edge of my bed and rests a comforting hand on my foot.

This is one of Tommy's numerous complexities. It's like when he knows you've been pushed too far, he'll stop all the pushing and simply hold on to you.

Tommy slides closer. "Seeing you like this . . . I hate it." He studies my face, all concerned-like. And it takes me back to eleventh-grade marine biology, when Ellie assigned our social circle aquatic identities.

"Jake's a dolphin. Because like Flipper, he'll rescue you. You're a starfish—"

"Sea star," I corrected. For the last twenty minutes Mr. Fox had explained the difference in detail, but Ellie had a habit of drifting off sometimes. "It's an echinoderm, same as the sand dollar, not the same as a fish."

"You're a nerd," Ellie said, a crooked smile on her face. "And a *sea star*."

"Why sea star?" For some reason I'd thought she'd pick a turtle or a frog, something common and not quite as beautiful.

"Because you're mutable," she said, proving she had been listening. "That's why you always do fine. And . . ." She scrutinized me. "You're also really bony." Which was a less flattering feature of a sea star.

"I'm a sea horse—"

At this I laughed. "Because you plan on being monogamous and mating for life?" Ellie had kissed at least two dozen guys during our spin-the-bottle phase, but unlike me, she had never longed for a real boyfriend.

"No," she said, something unreadable moving across her face. "Because I can easily die of exhaustion."

I should have asked her what she meant, but at the time, I only said, "And Tommy?"

"*Oh.* Obviously, a sea jelly."

After some research, I discovered this *was* obvious. Like a sea jelly swimming blindly through the dark sea, Tommy was relatively harmless unless provoked. But if provoked . . .

With this in mind, I still whisper the dreaded question, because I just have to know. "Does Jake . . . does he hate me?"

"Fuck, Sarah . . ." Tommy averts his eyes, which seems to be an answer of sorts. "Does that matter? You just said he didn't come to see you in the hospital. I've been here almost every week. Where the fuck has he been?"

Tommy stands, and all his warmth goes with him. He gets the package and brings it to me. "Open it."

I look out the window. The sun is down now, the bare trees swaying fiercely in winter's heavy wind. Even huddled against the cold, they are more alive than me.

"No," I say, feeling slightly stung. "Right now I just don't want to care."

"Good." He sounds relieved. "I'm pretty sick of you caring. All right?" He takes a few deep breaths; then he goes back to caressing my foot. "Let's just watch a movie. Something funny. You want to do that?"

I nod, knowing he's right. That I need to face the facts. Jake doesn't care about me. And I shouldn't care about him. But doing that isn't as easy as Tommy would have it be.

I make room for him on the bed, and stop myself from protesting when he wraps me in his arms. The movie begins, and for the next two hours we are simply Sarah and Tommy. Friends. Almost lovers. The only two left in a set of four.

After Tommy leaves, my sisters return, bearing signs of leftover popcorn in the corners of their perfectly flossed teeth. Mom disconnects me from Lifetime TV and wonders aloud about the unique smell in my bedroom, the one that often follows Tommy and his red eyes around, and reminds me of my appointment with Concerned Therapist on Wednesday, and asks why don't I get up and take a shower or something. Then she leaves me alone, and from the corner Jake's package beckons to me.

Will it always be like this? Will I always be that lame girl who loved that boy who never loved her back? Who can't be happy with what she has because of what she wants? What I've always had is Tommy. What I've always wanted is Jake.

I reach for the package, and, like Tommy, I try to gauge its weight. Then I sit with it on my thighs and stare at it. I think about the sea jellies, swimming in darkness, stinging blindly. And about Ellie's sea horse, fighting wave after wave of endless ocean.

And that bubble in my chest expands—waiting, threatening to suffocate me—but I control my panic by remembering what Ellie said. That I am a sea star. That I can change. Survive.

With shaking hands, I peel back one corner of the package and then the next. Soon the exterior wrapping lies on the floor. On my lap is a brown box. I open the box and peer at the contents inside. At first it looks like a jumbled mess, but I realize that's because my vision is blurred. It's blurred because I'm crying so hard. I take a few breaths to calm myself down, but it's useless. I can't control this.

Finally, I focus in on dozens of pictures—some Polaroids, others regular four-by-sixes—of me and Ellie over the last five years: at parties, at school, with different hairstyles and different clothes, glaring at each other and laughing, sleeping on sofas and floors and campsites, and dancing at proms and homecomings.

The box falls to the floor. Pictures scatter everywhere. I stumble to my bed. Bury my face in my pillow. Take that ball in my chest and suspend it in midair.

I repeat the word "stoic" for hours.

Finally I am calm enough to put the box back together. I take it to my walk-in closet and slide it so far into the darkness someone would have to build a tunnel to China to find it. Then I flick off the light and try to sleep.

17.

Us hurtling toward that last
memory: a Fourth of July squished
together on a patchwork quilt, the
sky exploding above your open
mouth, Dad's arm around Mom's
shoulder, the edge of your toes
pressed against mine.

Jake

AFTER. FEBRUARY.

Less than a week after Amber's visit, I'm called in to see Dean Schwartz. The office is dark, a grand display of masculinity, and there is a familiar smell, but I can't place it right away. It's only after Dean Schwartz has settled himself comfortably behind his mahogany desk that the smell links to a memory of another office similar to this.

In that memory I am twelve, and I sit beside my sister, who stares listlessly at the walls. My mother sits opposite us, closer to the shrink. His name was Bob, I believe, and he had gray hair and kind eyes. We went to see him for weeks. Mostly, Bob asked questions. Mom dabbed at her eyes, doing her best not to cry. Ellie stayed silent, and I tried to somehow make them both feel better—a smile for Mom, a goofy face for Ellie—but nothing worked.

The memory is too disturbing. I close my eyes and rub my hand across my face, trying to shake it off, but it lingers, as clear and present as that pain that I get sometimes.

"Mr. Meyers," Dean Schwartz says, clearing his throat, "it's been brought to my attention that you're struggling in your classes. I'm afraid your grades just aren't up to par. And according to your professors, you're barely in attendance." He pauses, lowers his voice, because this is how you approach such a delicate subject. "I understand you experienced a huge loss last semester. But it says here that you've repeatedly refused school counseling. Why is that?"

Because it's the most obvious and self-explanatory response, I say, "I don't need counseling."

He squints his eyes and nods his head, as if he understands yet respectfully disagrees. "Well, then . . . maybe what's best for you and your future is that you take a break? Clear your head. Give yourself some time to heal." He pauses to flip through pages in his manila folder. Then he stares at me from over the rim of his glasses. He's nearly bald except for a few patches of thin gray hair that sprout from random spots on his head. This, along with the grim expression on his face, makes him look like an unhappy owl.

"Well, what do you think?" He clicks his tongue, and I wonder if he's put out by my silence. If he prefers standing in a classroom, lecturing students, rather than dealing with issues of academic probation and life crisis and someone's sister dying. Someone's sister maybe, possibly, committing suicide.

When he leans forward, I notice his golf-ball cuff links. I try to imagine him on some green, his bare arms slightly burned despite the careful application of sunblock. He seems like the kind of guy who takes his time lining up a shot. Like he has the available headspace for all that concentration. I don't know why, but that fact alone says a lot to me about his life.

He lifts the stapler from his desk and clicks it absentmindedly. I fight the urge to pull it from his hand. That kind of behavior will get you suspended. "This is hard for you, isn't it?" he asks.

It's a stupid question, so I give an equally stupid response. "Life is hard, right?"

Dean Schwartz nods vigorously, like I've said something wise. He snaps my file shut and clasps his hands together. "Yes, life *is* hard. But we survive. We move forward. I'm sure you'll be fine after the summer's over. Nothing like a little sun and rest to set you straight. And you'd be surprised how time heals most wounds. It's a cliché because it's true, you know." He rises, and because it seems logical, I rise too.

At the door, he pats me awkwardly on the back, nodding his head the way guys do to each other. Then his gaze shifts just a little to the right. He seems elsewhere now, thinking of more pleasant things, like golf carts and wooden tees. Or maybe his thoughts are of what he must do next, the moment after I leave. All I know is that his thoughts are no longer with me.

THREE YEARS BEFORE.

I said, "You've got to talk to her, Mom. You've got to say something to her."

Mom sat across from me at the kitchen table, wearing her scrubs and smelling like disinfectant. Several gray strands hung loose from her ponytail. "What do you want me to say, Jake?" Her eyes drooped down to her hands. She rubbed the stem of her wineglass, dipped her finger into the liquid, and pressed the wet tip to the dark wood. "You know how your sister is. She's different." She paused, and for a second I thought she wanted to say more, divulge some new piece of information that might help me understand Ellie. But that was not the case. "Sometimes, she likes attention. A part of her wants to do things to shock us. If I talk to her now, that part will know her antics worked, and she'll just get more and more dramatic. That's not what either of us wants. This cutting thing is just the latest stage. It'll fade."

"But what if it doesn't?" I studied her, the dark bags under her eyes, the skin cracking across her palms.

She sighed, took another sip. "We've been through this before. The self-tattooing. The nose piercing. The running away. Remember she did that every other night last December? She's like that. She's . . ." Again she dipped her finger in wine and pressed it to the table. Two red fingerprints side by side. "She's still angry and probably incredibly confused. And she won't go to therapy. And the therapist said that's because she's not ready. I tried to force the issue. Remember? But she just got worse. She wouldn't talk about it."

"That was before, Mom. She was scared. She's fourteen now She's ready."

"Yeah?" She stood up, went to the kitchen counter, and grabbed her pack of cigarettes. "Maybe she's not. Maybe we just need to let it go for now. And maybe you," she said, turning to me, her eyes hard, "should just leave all of this alone. I know you think you understand what's going on, but you don't. You need to trust me, okay? I'm the mom here. When your sister is really ready for help, she'll ask." She grabbed the bottle, tucked it under her arm, and went outside to sit by the pool. I watched her for a while, even though I knew she'd dangle her feet in the water and smoke cigarette after cigarette until her bottle was gone. This was her after-work routine.

Eventually, I went to Ellie's bedroom. I didn't know why, exactly. I thought maybe I could talk some sense into her. A part of me expected that her door would be shut and that she wouldn't open it for me no matter how hard I knocked. But she wasn't in her room, and when I went into the living room, I found her sitting there in the dark.

She said, "I heard every word. You don't have to worry about me. I'm fine. And she's right, you know. I just want all that to be in the past. Why can't you let it be in the past, Jake?" She looked at me, tears gathered in the corners of her eyes, but I knew they wouldn't fall. She'd just stand at the edge of it, somehow able to hold it all in.

I sat down beside her, rolled up the sleeve of her striped shirt, and stared at the cuts on her arm, raised, ridged. Painful, red-puckered skin in different stages of healing. I looked at Ellie, and I knew that my eyes had welled up too. I found it hard to breathe. I said, "This is not fine."

She looked toward the kitchen. "You heard what she said,

Jake. She wants to forget everything that happened. She wants to make me disappear."

I reached for her hand, remembering her at age four, when she always wanted to hold mine but I never let her. "I think you're misunderstanding what she means. She feels like she's tried with you."

Ellie laughed. She said, "You know she bought me an extra-long robe to use when Sargeant's around? She tells me my shirts are revealing when they're not."

"That's not true," I told her. Ellie often had a way of misconstruing my mother's words and intentions. "She's just being protective. She's just taking precautions—"

"Then why bring Sargeant here at all? Why'd she get married again if she wants to take precautions?"

"She has to move on, Ellie. She has to . . ." I stalled out here. Explaining why our mother always needed to be married was beyond me.

"Why do you always defend her, Jake? Why can't you ask yourself why *we're* not enough for her?" Ellie pulled her hand back onto her lap and rolled down her sleeve. "And I'll tell you something, Jake. I don't care what she says; she blames me for what happened. I know she does." She stood. It was obvious she didn't want to talk about it anymore. I could have forced the issue, but I didn't. These conversations were just too hard.

She pointed to her arm and said, "I'll stop. Okay? I won't do this anymore." She walked to the hallway and paused. She didn't turn around, but I heard her say, "I'm sorry, Jake." Seconds later I heard her music blaring.

Alone again, I returned to the kitchen. I stood at the sliding glass door and watched my mom smoke cigarette after cigarette. I imagined each burning ember was a memory she hoped would disappear.

18.

It only takes an instant for
me to be back there with you.
"Oh, Ellie, I like to make you
laugh," you'd say, and I imagine
how that must have sounded
to my mother in the kitchen,
her hands submerged in soapy
water as she stared off into
the distance. But we were in
the family room. Me, floating
somewhere outside my body,
praying this time would be
different, hearing the nervous
sound of my laughter until your
hand found that place. Mom calls
private. Then the room went
silent. The only noise the sound
of your heavy breathing. And
me, pinned beneath the weight
of my fear, eyes glued to the
distorted length of Mom's
shadow, spilling into the hallway.

Jessie

BEFORE. AUGUST.

Thirty minutes after Lola left, I made my way downstairs, past my parents and my sisters still lying on the couch, and through the kitchen door. Outside, I stopped to let the heat wrap around me. It was a balmy night with a light breeze, a full moon hanging low in the dark sky.

I eased my way into the bushes beside the stairs, crouching low until I felt the dirt. I emerged a few minutes later with scraped palms, dirty hands, and Ellie's sketch pad. I stopped at the foot of the stairs to brush the dirt from my jeans. That's when I heard Sarah's voice behind me: "What are you doing?"

I spun around, the sketch pad hidden behind my back. She and Ellie stood a few feet away, watching me.

"Spying, Jess?" Ellie asked, an amused expression on her face. It was the first time she had really spoken to me since we kissed.

"What's behind your back?" Sarah asked.

"Nothing." I shuffled backward, felt the stairway just beneath my heel.

Sarah stepped forward, her face scrunching up. "No, you're hiding something, and why are you dressed like that?"

I looked down. I was still dressed in Lola's black leotard and leggings.

"Rob a bank?" Ellie asked, and again we made eye contact.

"It's just something Lola left me . . . for a project." I took step after step until I reached the door, my hand desperately seeking the knob.

"Jess, you're freaking me out," Sarah said. "What's behind your back?"

"Yeah, weirdo." Ellie skirted Sarah and hopped up the stairs. She stopped before me, placed her hands on my waist, and whispered, "Let me see, Jess."

Sarah laughed. "You're scaring her, Ellie. Look at her face. Just leave it. She can have her secret."

"Let. Me. Go," I whispered.

"You don't want me to let you go." Ellie's voice was dan-

CARMEN RODRIGUES

gerously low. "Do you?" She gripped my hips tighter. "Do you?"

I shook my head, because the truth was, I didn't want her to let me go. Not ever.

"Ellie, come on." Sarah watched from the grass below, amused. "Let her go. I'm totally going to pee my pants."

"I will," Ellie said over her shoulder, "when she shows me what's in her hands." She turned to me, her expression serious. "Show me."

Finally, I found the doorknob. The door swung open, just as Ellie reached for the sketch pad. Our bodies pressed together. I could have stepped back, but instead I held still. She did the same. When she pulled away, the sketch pad was in her hands.

"How did you get this?" Her eyes widened in disbelief.

"I—I don't know," I whispered.

"What do you mean, you don't—"

"Well?" Sarah now stood a step below. She peered over Ellie's shoulder, but the staircase was too narrow for her to see much of anything. "What is it?"

"It's nothing," Ellie said, slightly dazed. She handed the sketch pad back to me and gave me a little shove. "God. Go on, weirdo." Her voice had somehow resumed its typically bored tone.

I spun around and through the doorway, as Sarah called out after me, "Wait! I wanted to see."

"It was nothing . . . ," I heard Ellie say. Her voice lowered, the words a series of mumbles, followed by the faint sound of Sarah's laughter.

That night I climbed into bed early, tucking Ellie's sketch pad beneath my pillow for safekeeping. I listened to my family below—my parents and baby sisters finishing *The NeverEnding Story*, while Sarah and Ellie joked around in the kitchen.

The block was quiet. Old Mrs. Sawyer had turned out her porch light. And Mr. Lumpnick had just walked Molly down the street, stopping to sneak a cigarette by the fire hydrant as she sniffed for scents of friends or nemeses.

When the music for the movie's final credits rolled, the TV was turned off—Mom herded Mattie and Meg off to bed while Dad went into the kitchen to tell Sarah and Ellie to take it upstairs.

Minutes later, Ellie entered the room alone and found me reading the nearest book. From the bathroom came the definitive gurgle of water running through pipes, and Sarah singing.

"Reading?" Ellie asked, her voice neutral despite our previous encounter.

"Um, yeah." My plan was to seem busy until Sarah got out of the shower, but I wasn't exactly convinced this was enough to avoid the inevitable confrontation.

"Interesting?" she said.

"Um, yeah." The nearest book had been Sarah's SAT prep book, and so I added, "I want to give myself plenty of time to prepare."

I heard her unzip her overnight bag.

"So, not interesting?" she said. "You don't have to stare at the wall, Jess. We're both girls."

"I—I was reading my book," I said, but I lowered it slightly to prove I was perfectly capable of looking at her. She sat on Sarah's bed now, wearing only a pair of panties. Her nightgown was folded neatly beside her.

I lifted the book up quickly so that it blocked my view of her completely. But the image of her undressed stayed in my head.

A few seconds later she sat down beside me, the heat of her body pressing against my thigh. She was wearing the gown now, the hem just barely covering her upper thigh. She lowered my book and stared at me with intense eyes. "Is what you're reading or what you just saw more interesting than my journal?" Her voice was cold, the indifference replaced with a quiet anger.

"I . . . I . . ." I looked down, my eyes focusing on a tiny bleach stain on my blanket. "I'm sorry," I finally said, my voice unbearably hoarse.

She took the book and set it aside. "Look at me, Jess. Did you break into my house tonight?"

Slowly I raised my eyes to hers, afraid of what I might find. Her mouth was a straight line, but there was a slight quiver in her jaw.

I nodded. "Are you going to tell Sarah?" I asked. Her answer to that question was mostly irrelevant. I just didn't know what to say, and I wanted to steer her away from my reasons why and toward something safer: the consequences.

"You did it on your own?" she asked. "Or with Lola?"

I didn't want to lie to her, but I knew that if I told her it was Lola's idea, she'd go after her. That would only make things worse for all of us. So I said, "Just me."

She nodded and looked away. I studied her face, the dark bags beneath her eyes, her sharp chin, the thick streaks of eyeliner, which she wore even to bed. The silence stretched, just the sounds of our breathing, the water beating against the shower curtain, and Sarah singing.

Our fingers were near each other on the bed, and for some reason I let my hand inch forward until the very tips of my fingers rested on hers.

This brought her back to me. She looked down at our hands, and then at me. Her features softened, but only for a second. When she spoke, her voice was hard. "What are you doing?"

"I don't know," I whispered.

I wanted her to kiss me more than anything, and I tried to tell her that with my expression. Maybe she understood, because she leaned forward a little, her mouth open slightly.

Suddenly the water stopped, followed by the sliding rings of a shower curtain pulled aside. Ellie glanced at the wall; her lips snapped shut. She stood, everything about her closed off now, and said, "Isn't it past your bedtime?"

The words stung, even though I didn't believe she meant them entirely. She moved back to Sarah's bed and slipped beneath the covers. A minute later Sarah entered the room, smelling of Irish Spring. She glanced at Ellie, who was already turned on her side, her arm covering her eyes. "Okay if I turn out the light, Jess?"

I nodded. The light flicked off, and Sarah slid into the bed beside Ellie. Soon I heard the sound of Sarah's heavy breathing.

I stared at Ellie's back, her body eerily still, as if darkness had the power to pause all the earthquakes she felt inside.

Hours later, I made my way through the house to the sofa in the basement. There I sat and thought about Ellie, from the first time

I saw her on our front porch to that day in her bedroom. I had never felt this way about anyone until she kissed me.

You don't want me to let you go, she had said, and it was true. I didn't want her to let me go, but what did that say about me? About her? I could hear Lola's voice in my head, her two words repeating over and over again: *Fucking gay. Fucking gay.*

I didn't know what to do with those words, not yet . . . so I put a pillow under my head and tried not to think. But sleep never came, just question after question and the feeling that nothing would be the same.

19.

I can't believe we ran through the rain in our underwear. Well, I can't believe _you_ ran through the rain. I'll always run, but you, you're too scared to see the possibilities. But today I felt like you really saw them, and that made me feel less alone, like someone else could see the world the way I see it.

Sarah

AFTER. FEBRUARY.

Around midnight, Jess enters my room, sits on the edge of my
bed, and passes a cold hand across my cheek. When I don't
respond—not because I'm sleeping but because I don't have it in
me—she shakes my shoulder. Reluctantly, I open my eyes.

I can tell she's been crying. Her eyes are red, and strands of
blond hair cling to the wet spots beneath. The rise and fall of her
shoulders says she's trying to hold it back, but it doesn't seem
easy.

"What's wrong?" I ask.

She shakes her head like she doesn't know, but I can tell this
is a lie. I open my blanket, and she crawls underneath. We curve
in together, clinging to each other like when we were kids, afraid

of all the noises old houses make. I wrap my arms around her. Soon her shuddering turns into crying; she pushes her face into my pillow until her moans are stifled, her eyes squeezed shut.

I remember her at age seven—her hair in pigtails, her eyes so curious, that question always on her lips: *Want to play?* But that was before, when I was the best friend she ever had. Now the distance between us has made her unreachable.

"Jess?" I lean over her, shake her softly, and then with more force. "Please. Open your eyes. Talk to me."

When she does open her eyes, she says, "There are things you don't know about me, Sarah."

"What things, Jess?" I try to imagine any secret that can tear her apart like this, but her world is so predictable that I can't. "Jess, tell me."

She shakes her head, her gaze going blank as she retreats into herself. Minutes later, she says, almost numbly, "Some days, I just want it to all be over."

"No, Jess." It breaks my heart to hear her talk like that. "Please, don't say that. Don't ever say that."

She says, "I would never leave you, but it's how I feel. That's all. It's how I feel."

I want to tell her I feel the same way. That if I could, I'd take the first boat out of these floodwaters. That it's just fear keeping

CARMEN RODRIGUES

me in place. But I don't say anything. It's too hard to speak. All I can do is hold her until she is quiet—the weight of her sorrow drowning her in sleep.

Concerned Therapist shuffles around, checking her notes, lighting candles, muttering about breathing exercises and the importance of finding your center. She's a firm believer in finding your center. I bet each morning, before she drinks her organic green tea or waters her flowers or makes love to her husband, she sits cross-legged on a yoga mat and searches for the core of her being.

"It's important," she repeats, settling into her chair before putting her cell phone on vibrate, "to find your center." She turns to me and smiles that therapist smile that says, *I really see you. You're important.* Then she clears her throat and asks, "How are you feeling?"

I stare at the clock, watch that small hand spin by for a while, before I say, "Fine."

She nods, swallowing hard. "How are your sisters?" She angles her pen over her notebook, ready to write down anything even remotely relevant.

"Good," I say, but I think about Jess, how scared I felt for her, and I wonder what might happen if I told Concerned Therapist a little bit about it. The thought doesn't stick. Because I know if

I talk to her about Jess, she'll unravel the story, untwisting all its threads until they lead back to me. So I push it from my mind. I count to one hundred and twenty, because this trick buys me time. Then I say with a lot of effort, "Yeah, everything's fine."

The counting is another part of my avoidance technique. For the last six sessions, I've successfully dodged Concerned Therapist's questions with long silences and silly discussions: *Jess borrowed my shirt, and she didn't ask. That really upsets me. Mattie's really cute, but she's always the center of attention. It's really frustrating. Meg is so boy crazy it drives my dad crazy. I really hate to see him worry so much.*

Concerned Therapist consults her notes and picks, with almost superhuman intuition, the first name that pops off the list. "Is Jess still taking your clothes without asking?"

I think of Jess, with her frail frame and disinterest in anything. I wonder if she'll ever take anything of mine again. *We all have secrets.* That's what Tommy said. And it was true; we all did. Me, Tommy, Jake, Ellie . . . All of us had secrets . . . big, terrible secrets. But I never wanted that for Jess.

I'm getting worked up, so I think: *Stoic. Stoic. Stoic. Stoic. Stoic. Stoic. Stoic. Stoic.* And then I'm fine again. I'm back on track for therapy. "Jess just wants to talk about boys and life and stuff. I find it tiring," I say to Concerned Therapist.

CARMEN RODRIGUES

"And why does it bother you when your sister talks to you? Opens up to you?"

I count to one hundred and twenty before I say, "It doesn't bother me." And then I wait. It's a toss-up whether or not this was the correct response. If instead I had replied that it did bother me, I might have had a half-hour session on sibling rivalry. This would be preferable to moving on to some other topic that may or may not hit a nerve. To swing it toward sibling rivalry, I add, "I guess it's annoying."

Concerned Therapist stops writing, taps the tip of her pen on the top of her linen pants, and stares at me. This is the danger of Concerned Therapist. Even when you try to lead her down the wrong path, she somehow stumbles onto the right one. "Let's go with that. Why does it bother you when Jess cares what you think? When she wants to hear your opinion?"

"It dooon't," I mumble. And that's sort of true. A part of me wishes Jess would open up. But another part is glad she's pretending like last night never happened. It's taking all I've got to keep myself afloat.

"What's going on?" Concerned Therapist leans closer. Her perfume smells drugstore-bought, like an after-bath splash. It's a small detail, but it makes her seem more human to me. "Tell me what you're feeling."

One, two, three . . . "Nothing," I finally say.

"Are you sure?" Suddenly, we hear a soft bell, indicating someone has entered the waiting room. It's either my mom or the next client. Concerned Therapist checks her watch and realizes once again time has slipped away. I bet she wishes we could string these forty-five-minute sessions together like beads on a necklace. I bet she thinks that if we could, there'd be some sort of a breakthrough.

As if her superhuman intuition heard me, she says, "I'm going to talk to your mom about increasing our time together. I think we would make more progress if we had two hours to work with." But she says this nearly every time we meet. And every time, I nod my head like I agree, which I don't.

The truth is, I won't see Concerned Therapist for two hours a week—at least not by choice. When Mom broaches the subject, I'll tell her I'm doing fine. That I am much better than before. *Really, Mom. I promise.* And she'll believe me. Not because my words sound true, but because sometimes it's easier for us all to pretend.

CARMEN RODRIGUES

20.

You said, No, we can't press
charges. You don't want that.
You'll have to testify. You'll
have to see him again. The best
thing to do is to make him leave
the city. And tell him he can't
come back. And that'll be good
enough. And I believed you,
because at the time I didn't
know better. At the time, I
was too afraid.

Jake

AFTER. FEBRUARY.

I arrive in Miami with two carry-on bags and a weight in my chest. The bags are light, just the essentials: toothbrush, clothes, running shoes. The weight in my chest is heavy: Ellie's life, Ellie's passing, my longing for Sarah, my failure at school, my broken link to my mother.

After I exit the plane, I call my mom to tell her I've arrived safely. Her words are the same as before: "I just don't understand why you have to stay with your father. Why not Ohio? Or come here to Arizona. I love you, Jake. Your father loves you too, but he doesn't care about you like I do."

And like before, I don't tell her that that's the reason I've come to stay with him. Instead I say, "Mom, I'm fine. I'll call you soon. Okay?"

At baggage claim I'm greeted by my father, who gives me a slap-on-the-back hug, and his wife, Carla, who exclaims, "Oh, look at you!" And kisses me on the cheek.

Then there is the long fight through traffic on 826 West. My dad and Carla make small talk in the front, while Liza, my baby sister, sleeps soundly in her car seat, her thumb tucked warmly into her mouth. Finally, we arrive at a house crowded by palm trees. It seems like the typical South Florida construction: concrete walls, mango paint job, deep-brown roof tiles, and a paved driveway that curves around the yard like a question mark.

It's been a while, so I get the tour again: formal living room, dining room, family room with flat-screen TV. They take me out back to show me the inground pool. They say, "It's not like Ohio. Nearly every house here in Miami has an inground pool." When I bend over to touch the water, they say, "You'll get a lot of swimming done."

They walk me to my guest room, set my bags on the bed. Carla says, "It's so great you could come visit your home away from home." She pats me on the shoulder. And I think, *You do not visit a home; you return to a home*, but I don't say this. I just offer them a shaky smile.

Dad says, "We'll get dinner started. It's early by Miami standards—typically we don't eat until about eight—but we're sure you must be starving."

Soon the house is filled with the noise of their cooking. I lie on the bed and stare at the ceiling fan whirring above me, the sounds of its blades both hypnotic and comforting.

21.

This fantasy: you and me,
lying on my bed. Reading.

Silent but secure.

Jessie
BEFORE. SEPTEMBER.

The night before I went to Ellie's house to ask her about the sketch pad, I stood in my empty bedroom and practiced what I wanted to say. Mom had taught me this trick when I was five and scared to death of show-and-tell. *Just stand here, Jess, in front of this mirror, and say everything you want to say about that shell to yourself. Trust me. It'll help.*

And it had helped me conquer my fears about public speaking, but it didn't make it easier to stand in Ellie's doorway and see the bored expression on her face.

She didn't seem surprised to see me, not from the way she flipped the page of her magazine and said with a sigh, "Come in."

I entered the room slowly and stood over by her desk.

"How'd you get in?"

"Your mom." I pointed to my right, as if she might follow the invisible line that stretched between my finger and her front door.

"Obviously." She turned the page. "But why are you here?"

I set her sketch pad on her bed and backed away, unsure of her reaction. But she didn't react. She flipped a page and continued to read her magazine.

"I saw," I finally said. "I know you draw pictures of me."

That was an understatement. Ellie hadn't just drawn a few pictures of me; she had drawn dozens, in various states with various mediums—charcoal, pastels, ink—and some of them dated back to at least a year before.

She rolled onto her back, the magazine above her. "Yeah? And . . . ?"

I didn't know if I could trust my voice—my throat felt constricted, making it hard to breathe—but eventually I said, "I just think we should t-talk about it."

She closed the magazine, twisted her long blond hair around her fingertips. Her head rolled toward me, her eyes rimmed with their usual violent black eyeliner.

I tried not to let her stare intimidate me, by focusing on what I had practiced last night in the mirror. This time when I spoke, I didn't stutter. "Don't you think we should talk about how we feel?"

"How we feel?" Ellie's voice was dry, still distant. She unfolded her small body from the bed and stared out the window. I watched her. She seemed more interested in the neighborhood than me.

A voice inside me whispered: *You could just go. You could just walk out of here and never talk to her again.* But then Ellie closed her blinds and said, "Get the door, okay?"

I took a deep breath. This was what I wanted—a private conversation with her—but it still scared the heck out of me. "What about your mom?"

"Jess, even if you were a boy, my mom and the asshole wouldn't care. Really." To prove her point, she pulled a pack of cigarettes and the lighter with—I was convinced—Mattie's Hello Kitty sticker from her dresser. She lit the cigarette. "Well?"

"What about Sarah?" I asked, stalling.

"Please." Her tone was sharp. "I'm pretty sure she's somewhere with her head up Tommy's ass." She paused, her cigarette hovering.

She actually looked pained, and I wanted to touch her arm or maybe even hug her, but I didn't know how to close our gap. Instead I said, "I'm sorry."

"About what?" Her gaze wilted into a glare. She brushed her hair over her shoulder. Then she walked toward me, gliding her hand across mine as she passed. She shut the door. When she passed again, our hands locked. She led me to the bed, where we sat, our jeans touching—hers faded gray, and mine sensible navy blue. She put her cigarette out in a nearby ashtray. "Close your eyes."

The little voice whispered: *You can still leave. You could just go.* But another part of me, the part that wondered what came next, listened. I closed my eyes. Waited.

Her hand brushed my face, and, instinctively, I jumped. She laughed. "I like how you listen to me. You hear me, Jess," she said, her breath heavy on my skin. The next time she spoke, her mouth was only inches from my ear. "Go on, talk. I'll listen."

I opened my eyes and stared at her. I didn't want to say the words aloud. It was too hard to confess my feelings when I knew she'd never admit hers. She placed a hand on my knee and let it crawl upward until her fingers found the indent above my clavicle. After a second, she grabbed a strand of my hair and gave it a light twist. "Admit it," she said. "You really like me."

It was such an obvious fact; I didn't know why she needed my confirmation. "I—I—" I began, choking on my own spit. I turned my head away from her so I could cough.

She scooted away, our thighs no longer touching. I felt this ache, like a crinkling in the center of my heart. I was starting to believe that all of this—from our very first kiss to now—was a cruel joke, a game to pass her time.

"Well?" she said, her voice indifferent. And I knew that if I didn't say anything, I'd go back to just being Sarah's annoying little sister, and months might pass before she'd acknowledge my existence again.

"I . . ." Tears of frustration pooled in the corners of my eyes and started to seep out. "I like you, Ellie." The words stayed stiffly between us, and I realized that this was where it ended. She only wanted me to admit it, so she could turn on me the way she turned on Lola.

But then she looked at me, her face softer than before, her voice nearly gentle, and said, "You're crying."

I swiped clumsily at my cheeks, embarrassed by my tears. "I'm sorry."

"Don't." She knelt in front of me, pulled my arms down to my sides. "Don't." She traced the tears downward until her fingers rested on my lips. "I'm such a bitch, and you're not. You're so incredibly kind."

"I just want you to stop pretending. I want you to see me," I whispered, looking toward the square of bright light hidden behind the closed blinds. I wiped my face with the sleeve of my shirt. "I just—" Her hand slipped over my mouth and silenced me. She turned my face so that our eyes met.

She said, "I see you, Jess. I do." And then, very slowly, she kissed me.

22.

When I'm around you, I don't
know what I'm doing . . .

Sarah

AFTER. MARCH.

Mom drives me home from therapy. I change the CD, compulsively roll the car windows up and down, and in my head it's like my mom and I do this shuffle dance. We shuffle through songs. We shuffle through lights. We shuffle through the facets of our lives that are too disturbing for either of us to want to understand.

Mattie sits in the rear, belted into her car seat like some kind of porcelain doll with glass eyes that roll backward if Mom hits a speed bump too fast. I think Mattie is starting to understand. She's starting to realize that Big Sister isn't the same sister as before, and that even good families can turn silence into an art form.

"Your father will be home this weekend," Mom says. She

makes a left on Cherry Hill Drive and halts obediently at a stop sign. She looks around and then at me like she wants to touch me, but she doesn't. I continue to fiddle with my window. I roll it up and back down, wanting to drown in the sound of the wind coursing through her Ford station wagon.

"He wants us to do something as a family for spring break next week. Maybe take a trip. What do you think, Mattie? Would you like to take a trip?" Mom glances at Mattie's reflection in the rearview mirror. I think she's praying for some form of approval from the only friend she's got here.

"Can I bring Ann?" Mattie lisps through her mountain of missing teeth—the ones she has sacrificed to the tooth fairy in exchange for cash. She holds up the Raggedy Ann doll that has been passed down from sister to sister for the last thirteen years. "She wants to come."

"Of course, sweetie, of course. What do you think, honey?" Mom takes a deep, nervous breath. "Sarah?"

"I think"—my voice as distant as my heart—"the idea sucks."

"Well . . ." Mom makes a sharp turn onto Belvedere and stops abruptly at the light. She seems unsure of which direction to take. "I think it's a fabulous idea. Right, Mattie?"

Mattie says, "We like the cabin. Can we go to the cabin on the lake?"

"Oh, I don't know, Mattie," Mom says.

"But why not?" Mattie says.

Mom is silent. She's probably recalling that last year we took Ellie on our vacation there, and debating whether a return visit will be enough to push me to the edge, when the truth is I'm way past standing on the edge. Right now I'm clinging to it with the tips of my fingernails. "I'm not sure Daddy meant to go so far. The cabin's a long ways away," Mom says finally.

But I say, "I think I'd like to go to the cabin. It'll be warmer there." No ice. No snow. No Concerned Therapist. No Smith. No box in my closet digging its way to China.

"Really?" Mom says. "I guess it's a nice place to have some family—"

"Can I bring Tommy?" I interject before she gets on the subject of family time, which is the opposite of what I want. I want silence, crickets, Tommy acting as a buffer between me and her.

"Well, I'll have to ask your father about Tommy, but I think that'll be okay. It'll be fun. I promise." She winks at me, trying hard to be cheerful, but her face must not remember these kinds of gestures, because it remains stiff, her lips spread thin.

It feels like months since I've actually looked at her. Her disheveled hair hangs in a ponytail at the base of her neck.

She wears yoga pants and one of my dad's SEMPER FI T-shirts. I remember when we were young how she used to doll up—all high heels, trench coats, and patent leather purses. But lately, she is stretchy pants and running shoes. I wonder if she, too, had the ability to hurt her mother the way I always seem to hurt her.

"Are you okay, Sarah?" Mom is surprised by my gaze.

"I'm fine," I mumble. I look out my window, ignoring the reflection of her curious face. Her wide eyes blink quickly, like she's caught in a dust storm. "I said I'm fine." My voice is terse, and I start again on the automatic windows. I push the button and watch the glass move up and down. Now the car is silent, except for Mattie in the back, singing.

"It's going to be okay, Sarah" is what Mom finally decides on. "I just want you to know that." She places her hand underneath my elbow like she wants me to turn to her. But I can't . . .

I can't because I'm afraid if I do, some piece of my heart will break open. And the things I want to say will spill out and hurt us all. So I wait, and Mom waits too.

The light flashes green, and only then does she let me go.

23.

The morning you found out, you crushed me to your chest, and your tears wet my hair. Later you stood barefoot in the backyard, a trash can in front of you, a pile of his clothing at your feet, that bright flame licking the sky, all those white ashes rising up, swirling around you, like an SOS.

for such a good-looking kid. Why do you read so much?" They say, "Even at our old age, we've never read all these books."

The rest of my time is spent running past strip mall after strip mall. Some days, I walk the man-made canals that connect the housing developments with names like Panache and La Palma and Summer's Cove, and I think about what this world with its peach houses and always-green grass might hold for me.

But two months after I arrive, Carla stops eating her chicken and rice and stares at me across the dinner table. She says, "Jake, your father and I discussed it. We think it's time for you to go home and really deal with some of your issues." My dad is silent, his jaw clenched, but Carla nods toward him anyway. Liza sits across from me in her high chair, giggling, but Carla does not seem to see this. She says, "The depression isn't good for Liza. It makes her feel unsettled." Again, she looks to my father for support, but finds none.

Carla says, "You need to decide about school and your future. And being here is just delaying all that. Once you've figured it out, we can talk. We'd love to have you back for a visit, but we think it's important for you to take care of this now." She doesn't mention that this is supposed to be my "home away from home." I don't mention it either.

A few days later, my dad drives me to the airport. He doesn't

Jake

AFTER. MARCH/APRIL.

At night, when the palm-tree fronds brush against the roof tiles, I let my mind wander. I think about what life would be like if I stayed here forever, enrolled in junior college, let my dad be my dad again. I picture us working in the yard, sweat glistening off our backs, beers cradled in our hands. I think about watching Liza grow older, about always letting her hold my hand.

For whatever reason, these impossible plans alleviate the pain, save me from the boredom of days spent mostly in my bedroom, reading books from the library: *Far from the Madding Crowd*, *A Passage to India*, *On the Road*.

I have made friends with the blue-haired ladies who like to spend their afternoons in the library. They say, "You're too smart discuss his reasons for sending me back, but he hints at them. He says, "Carla's not used to stress." He says, "The baby has a routine." He says, "I'm sorry I wasn't there for you when you were little, but this time I've got to get it right."

Curbside, he avoids my stare. I don't know what to say to him, so I stand there with my hands in my pockets, waiting for something I'm not even sure is coming. Around us are honking horns and policemen directing traffic. Exhaust, heavy and acrid, coats our skin. The palm trees sway fiercely with the arrival of another afternoon storm.

Finally, my dad looks toward the American Airlines sign and says, "Ellie called me the day before she died. She said she wanted to come here, to live with me . . ." Then he looks at me. His eyes are red.

The words come out of nowhere, like a sucker punch to my chest. My body can only react. "Wh-what did you say?" I finally ask.

He rubs his hands through his hair, looks up at the sky. "I said I had to ask Carla, and I'd call her back." A few tears gather in the corners of his eyes, make it just to the tips of his eyelashes before his thick hands wipe them away.

"What did Carla say?" The noise around us is drowned out by the thumping in my chest.

"She said no." He blinks furiously, but no amount of blinking can stop this flood. Outside Terminal C of Miami International Airport, a wall has cracked. "I didn't know, Jake. . . . I thought . . . I thought we'd have more time."

He reaches out to me with the same hands that taught me about gardening and bikes and being a gentle older brother. I don't know what to do, so I take those hands, move a little closer, shield him from the prying eyes of others.

Inside the airport, I call my mother. She tells me how a few days ago she celebrated her third month of sobriety. She asks me about my semester of freedom (as she has decided to call it), if the sun in Florida has done me any good. She tells me that she's finally able to do the Bird of Paradise in yoga class. "You wouldn't believe how much balance that pose takes, Jake. When you come to visit, I'll teach you." We are silent for a bit, and then, like she does with each phone call, she tells me she is sorry, how she wishes she could change all the mistakes she's made, but she can't. "And I have to live with it."

I don't say anything to that, but because I am a dutiful son, I stay on the line when she starts her "aha moment." I take it all in, a safe place for her to store her regrets.

• • •

CARMEN RODRIGUES

In Smith, I sleep the weeks away. For the most part Gary leaves me alone, but I feel his presence. There are notes left in the kitchen, pointing to the meals delivered daily. There is money left on the coffee table in case I want to get out of the house and see a movie. A spring jacket, the kind used by runners, miraculously appears on my bed two days after I arrive, but when I see him, he doesn't mention it. He just says, "Are you sure you don't need to talk? When you're ready, I'm here."

Once Tommy realizes I'm at home, he stops by for a visit. It's only four in the afternoon, but already he's high. He says, "Why didn't you call and tell me you were coming? You should come by. Smoke out. Or have you gone all straight?"

I haven't spoken much to Tommy since I left for NYU, and that wasn't an accident. In some ways he's like a brother to me, but in others he's the worst friend I ever had.

I briefly tell him where I've been and what I've done and what I'm not doing anymore. The whole time, he's fidgety, moving around the kitchen and glancing across the yard toward his place. About ten minutes in, we hear the distant sound of someone knocking. I follow his gaze and see a girl as small and blond as Ellie standing in a thick jacket right outside his door.

Tommy says, "Whoa, dude, chill the eff out. Don't give me that look. It's donzo between me and Sarah. Been that way for a while now." He knocks on the windowpane, catches the girl's attention, and waves. "Yep, as over as that haircut you're rocking."

I say, "And what about her?"

He says, with a smirk, "What about her?"

After Tommy leaves, I go to the living room. I pull the curtain aside and watch Sarah's house. It's something I do a lot of lately.

Before Ellie died, the house was full of noise, but now their world seems muted. The curtains are always drawn. Mattie plays quietly in the yard. Jessie comes and goes, but she looks tired and underfed. Meg still runs wild, but she does it far away from the house. I have yet to see Sarah.

I think about what Tommy has said about him and Sarah being over, consider what that means. When it grows dark, I put on my gear and run.

24.

It was like hovering above
yourself, like stepping outside
of your own skin, trying not to
feel what's happening to your
body. It was over in minutes,
but I stayed outside, my spirit
freed from gravity, the earth
and Tommy so small behind me.

Jessie
NOVEMBER.

After Mom left to join Dad at the hospital, I put on *Bedknobs and Broomsticks* and sat with my sisters on the couch. Mom had loved this movie as a girl and would play it for us whenever we got sick or something terrible happened. When her mom died, years before, we watched *Bedknobs and Broomsticks* for what felt like weeks.

About twenty minutes into the DVD, Mattie fell asleep and Meg's eyes glazed over. I slid off the couch and went outside. The neighborhood was quiet again, the edges of the darkness slowly turning pink.

This time it wasn't hard to get in. Ellie's front door was unlocked. I stepped into the living room and noted everything out of place: the liquor-cabinet doors that were ajar, the empty bottle of gin lying on a table that had been bumped into the walkway.

The more I saw, the more anxious I felt. It took forever, but slowly I pushed forward, until I stood in her doorway. The room was a disaster—cigarettes scattered everywhere, Polaroids strewn across the floor, and in the corner a single white cap, the kind that fits a pill bottle. I moved closer to Ellie's bed, the smell of vomit suddenly hitting me like a train.

I ran back to the porch, gulping in the fresh air. The lump in my throat had grown to epic proportions, but still I could not cry.

In the kitchen I found a pair of rubber gloves, a sponge, and a bucket, which I filled with hot water, adding a cup of vinegar, just like my mom had taught me. Then I returned to the room, fell to my hands and knees, and began to scrub.

The front door opened and shut. A voice I hadn't heard in months yelled out, "Ellie? Ellie?" There was a pause. "Hello?"

Jake appeared at the door. He took in the room and me on my knees. "Jess, what are you doing? Where's Ellie?"

I stopped scrubbing, rolled back onto my heels, and said quietly, "There was an accident. Didn't your mom call you?"

His face contorted, almost like he knew this was much bigger than a fender bender or a slip-and-fall in the shower. "My phone's dead. I've been driving all night. What kind of accident? Where's Ellie, Jess?"

My words were quick, all sharp consonants. "Tommy called an ambulance. They're at Smith Memorial. My dad's there too. I don't know anything else. . . ." I didn't have the heart to tell him about Ellie. About it *not being good.*

He took in the room again, only this time slowly. His mouth opened, but no sound surfaced. Then he put his hand to his chest and held it there, tightly fisted. The veins in his neck emerged and spread upward, until one large vein seemed to split the center of his forehead. Again his mouth opened and shut. Still no sound.

"Jake?" I stood, rubbing my hands on my jeans. I wanted tears, but for some reason all I felt was that unreachable numbness—a fear I might never be able to find myself again. I took a step toward him. "You okay?"

He nodded, but his crimson eyes said the opposite.

"Jake," I said, "it wasn't just Ellie. It was Sarah, too."

It was just a split second before he turned away, but still I saw it, that next wave of pain that washed across his face.

Moments later the front door slammed shut, and Jake was gone.

• • •

When I finished cleaning Ellie's room, I emptied the bucket of water in the backyard and put away my supplies. Then I lit her favorite vanilla candle and placed it on the center of her dresser. I pocketed her Hello Kitty lighter and sat on the bed. Near my feet were the sketch pads, somehow still carefully stacked. Below me, hidden beneath her mattress, was the box.

Weeks before, Ellie had offered to let me go through her sketch pads. She said, "It's kind of like a visual history of me. If you ever want to know the truth, here it is."

"Like your own graphic novel?" I teased.

She smiled. Then she took a deep breath, like she was trying to get herself under control, picked up the stack, and laid it between us on the bed. There were ten. "I just want someone to know," she said.

I slipped my hand into hers, waiting to see if that was okay. When she didn't pull away, I asked, "Why, Ellie?"

"No reason." She leaned back against her headboard and closed her eyes. All the black eyeliner and eye shadow made it seem like her eyes had been cut out and all that remained were empty sockets.

"I hate when you do that," I said.

"You could take one now."

"What?" But I knew what she meant.

"Go on." She nudged me with her foot. I stared at her fishnet stockings. There were holes where the knees should be.

I felt tempted. I wanted so desperately to know more about her, but at the same time I wanted her to trust me enough to tell me what it all meant. I gathered the sketch pads and set them beside the bed. "I don't want to learn about you that way. I want you to tell me. Why won't you talk to me?"

She shook her head. "Do you think I should dye my hair black? It'd look cool with my blue eyes."

"I like your hair blond. It's the same color as mine." She opened her eyes, and something inside me jumped, surprised as always by their intensity. "You want to be different from me?" I moved beside her and rested my head on her shoulder. "We're the same. We're the only two I know that are the same." I picked up a strand of her hair and placed it against mine. "See? They're almost identical, so we must be the same."

She laughed. She always laughed at me, but not like everyone else did. Her laughter made me feel special, like she got me.

"You should go." She picked at her stocking, so that it tore right above her thigh. "Sarah and Tommy are coming over soon."

"So?" I hated when she made me leave.

"So? So?" She stood up and walked to her desk, separating

herself from me. "They can't know. You know that." She picked up her black eyeliner and started lining the inside of her eyes. She turned to me. Her expression changed. "Go already."

It was useless to fight with her when she got like this. So after grabbing my backpack from the floor, I came up behind her and wrapped my arms around her waist. "Ellie, why won't you tell me?"

"There's nothing to tell." She stepped away. "Just go already."

This was the pattern with her. She'd pull me close only to push me away. But with every tug-of-war I felt her guard slipping, and I consoled myself by saying it was only a matter of time until she let me in. One day she would pull that secret box from under her bed and show me.

But she never did. So I knelt in her bedroom, the scent of vanilla flooding the air, and took it.

That night Mom entered my room and found me awake, staring at nothing in particular. We had spoken briefly that afternoon, but our conversation had been short. Just long enough for her to say Sarah's situation seemed promising, that she hadn't heard anything else about Ellie, and to remind me of Meg and Mattie's nighttime routine.

Now she sat on my bed and gave me a firm hug. She smelled

like hospital and coffee. "So the good news is, Sarah's stabilized. The doctors say she'll be fine eventually, but it'll be some time. Dad's going to stay with her overnight."

I moved my gaze to my hand resting on the comforter. I had done my best during the day not to think about Ellie, but it was hard not to worry or imagine what was happening to her at the hospital. I had seen enough of *Grey's Anatomy* to know they had probably pumped her stomach, given her fluids, and monitored her condition carefully. I hoped she wasn't in a lot of pain. But whenever I started writing lectures in my head about her being more careful and dealing with whatever was stuffed into that box, I turned my attention to Mattie and Meg and the mindless DVD playing on the TV.

It wasn't that I didn't care—I cared to the point that I hadn't been able to eat all day and I'd had to ask Mattie and Meg to repeat everything they said—but thinking about the aftermath made everything feel too real, and I wasn't ready for that.

So the day had passed, the lump in my throat nearly suffo-cating me, but somehow I had survived.

"And the bad news?" I finally asked, my hand trembling. I looked at her. It was there in her eyes. "How?" Even though I knew, I needed to hear her say it.

"Overdose . . . accidental, probably." She brushed my hair

behind my ears. "Are you going to be okay? I know you two weren't very close, but still . . ."

I nodded, unable to trust my voice, the world, and everything inside it. All my worst fears were happening—I understood that—but at the same time I felt so distant from it. As if I were floating away from Mom and her words, nothing above or below to anchor me.

My voice was weak. "I just . . . can we talk about this tomorrow?"

"Okay." She kissed my cheek before bringing me close for another tight hug.

After she left, I stared out my bedroom window, trying to hold on to any sense of reality. For a while there was only stillness inside me, an emptiness that ached. But slowly, very slowly, all the thoughts from the day and from every moment before with Ellie filled that space. That's when the tears finally came. I couldn't make them stop. For once, I didn't even try.

25.

I could spend all day with your
head on my belly, your breath
falling into me.

Sarah

AFTER. MARCH.

Days and days later, we are at the cabin, the sounds of utensils politely clicking away. Mom circles the table, refilling pitchers of tea and water, touching my dad's shoulder to reassure herself that she isn't alone in this chaos. Meanwhile, Dad tells us stories, cuts his meat with his manly knife, and smiles benevolently at us.

And here is Jess, sitting across from me, swirling her food around her plate, turning it into a Monet or something. And here is Meg, to my right, giggling and kicking Mattie's foot underneath the table. And here is Mattie, to Jess's left, with her fork perched awkwardly in her hand, her steak and potatoes drenched in ketchup. And here is Tommy, next to me, his hand underneath the table, crawling up my skirt until it finds the edge of my panties.

And here are my parents, still chattering, still fussing, still oblivious.

And here is me, pushing Tommy's hand away, the bubble in my chest expanding, not bursting. Waiting.

After my parents fall asleep, Tommy sneaks into the bedroom I share with Jess and hands me an unlabeled glass bottle filled with vodka. We slip out my window and head to the lake, passing the bottle back and forth in silence.

The walk is long. The water is ice cold. But still, we strip naked and slide in. Tommy grabs me, kisses me, but I'm not in the mood, so I swim as far away as I can. I float on my back, stare at the sky above dotted with stars.

This is where Tommy finds me. His face seems serious as he pulls me toward him, trying to wrap my legs around his waist. I push away and say, "Hey, I just want to swim."

He treads water beside me, the frustration evident in his voice. "What's your deal? You invited me here. You're—" He points at my nakedness; his expression completes the thought.

And he's partially right. I did invite him here. I did strip off my clothes. But that doesn't mean I want *this*.

I splash water at him, some juvenile attempt to lighten the mood. When he doesn't laugh, I dive under and try to force my body to come alive in these frigid waters. But I don't get far before Tommy grabs my waist and propels us onto the muddy bank.

"Come on, Tommy . . . Why can't we just swim?"

He tosses my clothes at me and starts pulling on his. I see he's angry, so I move a safe distance away. After I've got my jeans and T-shirt back on, I say, "I just wanted to have fun. I don't see why this is such a big deal."

"Is this fun to you?" He looks at me, furious. "'Cause this isn't fun for me."

"Tommy." I take a few tentative steps forward, touch his arm, but he pushes me away. "I don't know what you want from me." They're the same words we always come back to.

"Fuck, Sarah, it's not complicated. I just want to be with you, really be with you."

But it's complicated for me. "I don't even know what that means" is all I can say.

"It means"—his voice is clipped—"that you're all-in *with me.* Us in an actual relationship. Not this other bullshit where I don't even know half the time if I'm allowed to touch you." He waits for me to say that this is what I also want, but I don't. "But you're not in." His eyes are hard, with just a hint of sadness. "And you're never going to be, are you?"

Maybe it's because I'm exhausted and being with him feels even worse than being alone, but finally I tell him the truth. "No, I'm not."

He shakes his head, a low growl deep in his throat. "I just can't do this with you anymore. You never wanted me. You always wanted Jake. And you know what the crazy thing is?" His voice rises as he finishes yanking on his clothes, reaching down to grab the bottle of vodka. "Jake never wanted you. That's why he never fucking called you when you were in the hospital."

"That's not true!" I say, but instantly I know it is.

"And he just used you. He used you, the way you used me—"

"That's not true either, Tommy!" But again, my words ring false.

"Yes, it *is*." He turns and glares at me. "And I guess that's what we all fucking do. We use each other."

It's like he's throwing knives at me, each word slicing me into smaller and smaller pieces. All I can do is watch myself bleed, but then, as if it's an instinct, I turn all of this ugliness back on him. I say quietly, "Is that what you did to Ellie? Used her?"

The question is as honest as his accusations, but it's also vindictive and filled with enough implication to silence him.

From the way he stares at me, I can tell I flung that knife so hard it hit bone. His voice shakes when he finally speaks. "Fuck you, Sarah. Okay? *Fuck you.* I know what you're saying, you *fucking* coward. You were there that night. *Not me.* Don't you dare put that on me."

He charges toward me, his arm raised. I close my eyes, preparing for the inevitable blow. But it never comes. Instead there is a whooshing to my right, followed by a loud *pop*. I reopen my eyes. Tommy is gone, the bottle of vodka shattered beside me.

Alone, I collapse onto the earth—the certainty of Tommy's words cutting me over and over again.

26.

I never meant to hurt you.
Did you mean to hurt me?

Jake
AFTER. APRIL.

It's spring already, but the cold and drizzle continue. Tonight seems even colder and wetter than last night. I pull my scarf up over my chin and wait a few minutes. Then I pick up another stone and throw it at Sarah's window.

A light goes on, but when the window slides open, it's Jess's face pressed against the screen. She looks down at me in confusion. I don't know if she recognizes me, so I step into a circle of floodlight from the garage, tilt my head up, and pull off my cap.

She closes the window. The light goes off, and seconds later, downstairs, another turns on. A window opens. Jess sticks half her body out through the square, her blue eyes swimming in her gaunt face. She says, "Come on, I'll pull you in."

It's a ridiculous offer. "Why can't you open the kitchen door?" I ask.

"My mom locked it with a key, and she's sleeping." She juts out her hand. "Come on."

"Jess, there's no way. Move back."

I jump, pulling myself across the wet surface with barely any struggle. The house is warm. I take off my gear and look around. I'm standing in their den.

Jess leaves the room and returns with a kitchen towel. She bends down and starts to wipe up the puddle that's forming beneath my feet. She wears a thin sweater. As she works, her shoulder blades protrude from underneath. Without looking up, she says, "Sarah's in the basement. She's been there since Mom went to bed."

I step to the left so I'm out of her way. "Why?"

"I don't know. When I went to check on her, she told me to leave her alone." She takes one last swipe at the floor and stands. Her eyes are worried.

"Is she okay?"

She shakes her head. "Last night Mr. Lumpnick was walking his dog, and he found her just sitting in the middle of his sidewalk with nothing but her pj's on. She was freezing, and her arm was bleeding. . . . She said she must have cut it on a branch or something. That's why Mom changed the locks." She looks away. "Just go ahead. You'll see. Be quiet, though, or you'll wake my mom."

The basement door is slightly ajar, and I follow the light until I'm standing at the base of the stairs. The space is just as I remember—sofa, lounge chairs, and foosball table—but no Sarah. I move toward the light, calling her name, but I get no response. Dozens of thoughts race through my head. *Why did I never call her? Why didn't I let Ellie hold my hand when we were little? Why have I never told Sarah that I love her?*

I spin around. The laundry-room door is cracked. I move closer, push it open entirely. There she is, wearing only a slip, her hair falling in knots around her face. She raises a bandaged arm to shield her eyes from the light, and I see that her skin is pale, her lips chapped.

The sight of her is more than I can bear, but still I manage a shaky smile. I crouch before her. "Hey . . ."

She stares at me for a long while, her eyes filled with uncertainty. "Jake?"

"Hey, Sarah . . ." She resists, but I manage to gather her into my arms. The basement is so cold, but her skin feels like fire against mine.

"What are you doing here?" she asks.

"I—I needed to see you."

"But why . . ." She tries to pull away, but she's weak and her attempts feel more like a shudder. I hold her tighter until she gives in. "I thought . . . and you never called . . . and I waited for you all this time—"

"I know, Sarah—"

"Just tell me . . . Just tell me why . . . ," she whispers.

This is what she always does, looks for reasons to forgive me. But there isn't one. I ran because I was too afraid to face her. Too afraid to face myself. I thought it'd be easier to leave all this behind, to find a new home. But here with her, I realize that home is the place you return to when you can't run anymore.

27.

You make lists to connect
the spaces between me and
you. You think I'm good.
But I'm not.

Jessie

AFTER. APRIL.

"When did she start sleeping in here?" Jake guides Sarah to the bed and covers her with blankets. He glances around the room with swollen eyes, and if I didn't know him—the little that I do—I might think he spent the last twenty minutes downstairs crying.

"Mom thought she might want some privacy," I explain.

"That's the last thing she needs. She was practically naked when I got down there. She says she's cold, but she feels warm." He looks up at me like this is my fault. But it's not. It's just a ball that keeps rolling because nobody knows how to make it stop. "Doesn't your mom see what's going on?" His shoulders are tense, his hands balled at his sides.

"Jake, it's not her fault," Sarah says.

I stare down at her, so small beneath the blankets he's piled on top of her. Just like he said, she's shivering, but her face is wet with sweat. "Mom's seeing her doctor tomorrow and then they'll decide," I tell him, repeating nearly verbatim what my mom told me today. "Do you feel okay?" I ask. I touch her forehead. "You've got a fever. Maybe I should wake Mom."

"Yeah," Jake says, his expression grim. "Maybe you should."

Sarah pushes her tangled hair away, and sits up in the bed. "No, don't. I just need sleep, that's all. I don't feel that bad, really."

"I don't think that's a good idea, Sarah," Jake says.

"No," Sarah says, "I just . . . please . . . I'll feel better if I sleep."

"I don't think she's slept in days," I tell him. I know this because lately I can't sleep either, and throughout the night I hear the sounds of her restless movements below.

"You sure?" Jake asks, his reluctance audible.

Sarah nods and slips back down in the bed, pulling the covers up to her chin. "Can you get me water?" she asks.

I nod, and Jake follows me to the kitchen. I fill a glass and hand it to him.

He says, "I want to stay with her. Make sure she's okay."

I remember his face that day in Ellie's bedroom. "Okay."

"It's just . . ." His voice halts, realizing I've said yes. The lines and wrinkles disappear. For a minute he looks so much like Ellie it twists me up inside. "Thanks, Jess."

"My mom gets up at six, so you should be gone by then. Okay?"

"Okay," he says. He takes the glass back to Sarah's room. This time I follow him. I stop at the doorway and watch as he sets the glass down on the bedside table and helps Sarah into a sitting position. When he holds the glass to her mouth, waiting patiently for her to sip, I shut the door, because I can't watch anymore. It's too much to see everything I've lost.

BEFORE. NOVEMBER.

I found her lying on her bed in a robe, iPod cradled to her chest as she mouthed the lyrics to some song. Her eyes were closed, her wet hair twisted up in a towel. It was the first time I had seen her without makeup, and she looked young, slightly vulnerable, her face dotted with light brown freckles, her bare lips pink and glossy.

When I sat down on her bed, her eyelids fluttered open, her mouth twitching into a half smile. She removed the buds from her ear.

"Hey," she said, her voice mellow. "How'd you get in?"

"Caught your stepdad on his way out. Is your mom still out of town?"

"Yep," she said with a smirk. "Till Saturday. And as an extra bonus, he'll leave on Thursday to join her."

"Lucky you. What are you listening to?"

She held up an earbud. "Guess."

Lately we had mysteriously grown closer, as if Ellie had decided to wave her white flag in surrender. There was a rhythm to us now. We saw each other regularly—even if it was still kept pretty secret—and texted a lot. She was even teaching me about her favorite bands.

"Well?" Ellie said.

It took a few seconds to identify the lyrics. "Mumford and Sons?"

"You got it." A slow smile spread across her face. Her eyes were droopier than usual, as if she had been sleeping.

"Did I wake you?"

She shook her head, and put my hand on her waist, an unusual gesture from her. Most days she had to warm up to me first. But with this small encouragement and all the others accumulated over the last fourteen days, I decided to be brave and let my hand slip beneath her robe.

She laughed. "You're sassy today."

I shrugged, knowing she'd appreciate a vague response, and, watching her eyes carefully, I began to explore her. "Where were you last night? I texted you."

This time she was the one to shrug. "Doing something, I'm sure." She yawned.

"Why are you so sleepy?"

"You'll get mad if I tell you."

"No, I won't."

"Yes, you will." She pushed my hand higher so that it cupped her breast. A tingling sensation spread through me.

"Are you trying to change the subject?"

She nodded, reaching up to kiss me.

"Why are you acting so strange?" I settled in beside her, resting my head on her shoulder. I tossed one leg over both of hers and squeezed tightly. She called this my "monkey on a vine" move. "I won't be mad," I whispered, kissing her neck and then the center of her chest.

"Fine," she sighed. "You're lying. But fine."

I waited, because everything with Ellie was about waiting—each encounter some sort of pop quiz on patience and endurance. If anything, our time together taught me I could take a lot, but it was never easy.

She reached for a decorative pillow resting along the wall, unzipped the casing, and pulled out a small bottle. She handed them to me.

"What's this?"

"Some pills my mom threw out a few weeks ago."

I read the label. "OxyContin. They're expired."

"I know," she said. "And nearly full."

"Why did she have them?"

"Hurt her back last year, I think." She laughed sluggishly. "Can you believe she was just going to toss them? What a waste."

I had heard about this side of her from school, but I had never seen it. "How many did you take?" I kept my tone casual so she'd feel comfortable telling me. But she could hear the tension in my voice.

"Oh, come on, Jess." She fell back against the bed, and the towel on her head rolled open. Her hair was twisted up in a bun, the color so black it was nearly purple.

I stared at her. "What did you do to your hair? I thought we agreed you wouldn't do that."

"Oh my God." She hopped off the bed. She sat at her desk and began to brush her hair violently. Minutes later she set the brush down, spun around, and said, "FYI: You're being a priss-bitch again."

The words hurt, and I could see that white flag being lowered. Soon she would gather it in her arms, fold it corner by corner into a tiny, neat square that would be hidden away. "Why are you being like this? Did you have a fight with somebody?"

"Obviously." Ellie laughed. "Because I fight with everybody. Is that what you're saying?"

"With who?" I asked, knowing better than to be distracted into a conversation about what she did or didn't always do.

"Who cares?"

"With who, Ellie?"

"My stepfather, okay? God."

"When?"

She rolled her eyes. "I don't know. Yesterday. Today. All week. What the fuck difference does it make? You can't fix this, Jess. You can't fix me. So stop trying."

"Is that why you didn't text me back yesterday?"

Her face closed off entirely then. She swiveled around and began brushing her hair again.

"How many did you take?" She could avoid answering my question about the text, but this I needed to know.

She shrugged her shoulders. "Are you deaf? Why do you give a fuck about this?"

"Because I do."

"I was just testing them out—"

"What does that even mean?"

She hesitated for a second. "I don't know, okay?"

"How many?"

She slammed the brush down. "Two, okay? Why do you fucking care?"

I sat next to her, put my hands on top of hers, trying to calm her. "Please don't talk to me like that."

"Jess, you're so confused." She pulled her hands away from mine.

"No, I'm not confused. I'm not." I leaned over and tried to kiss her, but she shoved me away.

"You're acting crazy."

"I'm not," I said, the tears gathering.

"Are you actually going to cry now? Oh, you're kidding me. You're like some sort of goody-goody. How can you ever understand me?"

It was those last words that made me do it. I went for the bottle and uncapped it, dropping two pills into my palm.

"What are you doing?" Ellie asked. "Stop it. Just stop it."

I popped the pills into my mouth, swallowing quickly. Ellie grabbed my face, squeezed my cheeks so that my lips puckered together painfully. "Spit them out," she said. "Spit them out!"

I twisted away from her. "Too late. You want this. Then I want this. That's how it works."

She took a step forward. I thought she was going to hit me, but she grabbed my arm and dragged me to the bathroom. I fought her the whole way, but despite her stature she was way stronger. She shoved me to the floor in front of the toilet. Then she knelt down beside me. "Open your mouth," she said, but I ignored her. "Open your mouth, Jess!" She sounded like a parent, like if I didn't listen to her, she'd count to three and then who knows what. "Jess," she said, "you don't know what you're doing. You're going to get hurt like this. Is that what you want?" She waited for me to speak, but for once I let the silence settle between us.

"Fine." She stood up. A few seconds later her bedroom door slammed shut. I knew I should go after her, but I couldn't make myself move. It was quiet for a bit, but then I heard this mournful kind of wailing, a sound that should never belong to a human being.

I got to my feet, every part of me shaking, and made my way to her room.

She was naked, sitting on the bed with her bare back to me. She was bent over, something silver in her hands.

"What are you doing?" I moved closer, and that's when I saw her hand move swiftly, the slice of a blade across her thigh, and then blood, bright and thick. "What are you doing?" I shouted. She was sobbing now. I took the blade away from her and ran to the bathroom to get a washcloth and some peroxide from underneath the sink. When I returned, she was curled up in the fetal position on her bed, the blood seeping into the sheets. I cleaned the wound as best I could and held the cloth to her skin to stop the bleeding. Telling her the whole time that everything would be okay.

"But it's not," she kept saying. "It's not."

"Yes, it is."

I started to feel the OxyContin. My mind seemed to ease away from itself, the worries still there but not my ability to care. I wondered if it felt the same to Ellie, if that was why she took them in the first place.

The bleeding had stopped now. I wiped the remnants of it from her naked body, the washcloth passing line after line of old cuts. I began to cry softly. When I stood, Ellie whimpered, "Don't leave me."

"I'm right here," I said. I undressed quickly until we both wore only our histories—hers mutilated, and mine uninterrupted until now. I crawled into bed, curved my body around hers, and whispered, "Let's sleep, Ellie. When we wake, everything will be better."

28.

You have everything I ever wanted.

Sarah
AFTER. APRIL.

The next morning, Jake is gone, and I have to convince myself that he was really here. That I didn't imagine him. That I'm not as far gone as I think. And after a while, I'm able to believe in the memory of waking beside him in the night, his hand running up my thigh until it rested in that indent between my waist and hip.

"Are you okay? How do you feel?" he asked.

I twisted around, too sleepy to find words, the noise in my head down to a soft rumble. "Yeah, I'm better, I think."

"Sleep some more. You're exhausted." He pulled me closer, until my head lay against his chest, and caressed my back with tentative hands. I tried to relax into him, push away the millions of questions flooding my head. There were still no answers, still no reasons why. The only concrete thing was his presence in my bed. But maybe that was all that mattered. Maybe just for the moment we both needed to forget. I reached up to kiss him, but he was hesitant. "Jake, it's okay. I want this." I kissed him again, this time peeling up his undershirt until my hands lay flat against his abdomen. His skin was warm, taut. I slid my hands higher, running them over his flesh like it was familiar to me, when, really, I had never treated his body this intimately before.

"Sarah, wait," he said, but I continued touching him. "Sarah, I just want to hold you." He wrapped his hands in my hair, his breath as shallow as mine. "I can't."

It wasn't the worst thing he had ever said to me, but it hurt all the same. It was our song and dance. He didn't want me. He didn't know what he wanted. Or he didn't think he could give me what I wanted. "Why did you come?" I asked.

"I just needed to see you."

"So you see me," I said, my hurt turning into anger. I tried to pull away, but he held the length of me, keeping me still. He buried his head in my neck and whispered, "Please, Sarah. Don't, okay? I just need time . . ." His voice cracked. He stopped talking and held me tighter, his face hidden from my sight.

I rubbed his back. I knew how hard it was for him to say even that much, but I needed more. "Promise you won't disappear on me. . . ."

He nodded, his breath ragged. "I promise. Okay?"

But the next morning, like always, he was gone.

I take deep breaths, searching for my center like Concerned Therapist has taught me. But all I find are the things I have lost: my friendship with Jessie, the way Mattie used to trust me, the way Meg used to look up to me, the way my parents believed in me.

I find myself back in my bedroom, the room soaked in Jake's scent. I stare at the tangled sheets, and a deeper loneliness takes root.

I miss Ellie. I miss everything that was our Before. And for that reason alone, I dig a hole to China. I open the box, slowly taking out photos: Ellie in her *Mork & Mindy* T-shirt and me, looking slightly unsure, that flower tucked behind my ear; Ellie helping me blow out the candles on my sixteenth birthday; Ellie the week before she died, her hair as black as Snow White's.

The bubble in my chest is full now. The pain is so great I run from it. I run until I'm in my parents' bathroom, my face pressed to the cold tile floor. But the pain follows, and all these voices surround me.

I have a secret. Jake never wanted you. You just kept throwing yourself at him. Some days I just want it to all be over. I promise.

Just let me stay. Jake used you, the way you used me. We use each other.

I stare at my bandaged arm, the cut hidden beneath it the work of a jagged key. And I know there is only one way to make this pain stop.

There's time, I hear Ellie say.

I'm barely able to breathe as I grab my father's shaving kit from below his sink. I pull the straight razor free, taking everything that is dark inside me and silencing it with that first jolt of pain.

A thin stream of blood rushes down my palm, drips off my fingertips, and settles into the grout. I close my eyes, and Ellie is there. Purple pills raining down on us. The bubble in my chest ripping my skin, eager to get out.

I lean my head against the cabinet, tug the blade deep into my flesh. The blood streams out now, pools onto the floor. I fall onto the tile. The dusty sea of lost things beneath my parents' claw-foot tub fades into Ellie twirling and singing, *I have so many secrets, but I won't tell you.* The room twirls with her.

Sarah, catch up. Sarah. Sarah. Sarah.

My body grows colder and colder. And still, through it all, Ellie calls my name.

29.

Do you remember how we moved
in tandem, my arms wrapped
around your waist, my head
hidden underneath the back
side of your shirt? You baked
pies and sang and I found
that dimple above your hip bone
and told it the secrets of my
day . . . of fingers stained
red with finger paint, of a
recess spent chasing the girl
with floppy hair and murky eyes.

You were thirty-six then, and
you loved him.

Jake
AFTER. APRIL.

I am covered in Sarah's blood. That's why I am sitting here, in the hospital's designated smoking area, talking to a detective. All I want to do is smoke my cigarette, but it's hard to smoke when your hands are shaking so bad.

"I just want to know if she's okay," I say. In response, the detective jots something onto his notepad and nods. He's a large man with deep-set eyes and spotty gray hair. He slides an ashtray across the picnic table and says, "I just need to write my report, okay?"

An ambulance screeches to a halt outside the emergency-room doors. The detective watches it unload, his eyes automatically tracking the medics' movements. When the patient's inside, he says, "You're not in trouble, Jake."

I put out my cigarette. "I don't care about that. I just want to know if she's okay." I pick a piece of dried blood from the fabric of my sweatpants and set it on the picnic table. I consider returning to the ER's front desk, demanding that the nurse give me a logical reason why I can't see Sarah, why they won't provide me with any new information. "I just really need to know, okay?" My voice rises, and the detective shoots me a look in response.

"Son, you're going to have to stay calm; getting excited isn't going to help your friend—"

"I'm calm." I lower my voice. "But she's more than a friend, okay?"

"Son, I know you're frustrated, but rules are rules. The hospital can't release any information on your friend's condition if you're not a family member—"

"But I'm the one who called the ambulance—"

"And that was a good thing. You might have saved your friend's life."

I flinch at the phrase "might have saved." The detective's voice grows softer. "You'll find out more. I promise. Now let me do my job, okay?" The detective taps his pen over his notepad. He's only interested in facts, and so I give him the facts. As I speak, the pounding in my head grows, and over it is a loop of Sarah's voice asking me to not disappear. And when I close my eyes, there is a flash of her lying on her parents' bathroom floor, her nightgown soaked in blood.

"How did you know?" The detective leans in, real curious. "How did you know to go inside when she didn't answer the door?"

"I was worried. She doesn't leave her house, really—"

"How do you know that?" he asks, and even though he says I'm not in trouble, his voice is wary.

"Because . . . ," I say, and I tell him about the night before, how I was there with her, how I left because I didn't want her mom to find me there in the morning. How I went for a jog. How her mom's car was gone when I got back. Halfway through, my voice halts like a train that's hit a wall. A pain shoots through me, stretches from the top of my head to the tips of my toes. It's the same pain I felt with Ellie. I sit on the picnic bench and try to steady myself. I put my hands over my eyes, run them through my hair. I take a moment to breathe. "I should have never left."

The detective reaches out, pats me awkwardly on the shoulder. "Ain't no one to blame for what she did. She's just in a lot of pain. Now you just take a minute for yourself, okay?" He stands. "You just sit tight."

He walks briskly toward the emergency-room entrance, disappearing behind the double doors. I lay my head against the picnic table. I open my mouth, breathe in and out, watching the air turn into fog. The loop in my head grows stronger. It says, *If I need you, you'll come back for me?* It says, *Don't disappear.*

And underneath the loop is the sound of someone in a lot of pain. It is the sound of someone crying.

30.

I don't believe you when you
hold my hand and say you never
want to let me go.

Jessie
BEFORE. NOVEMBER.

I woke to Ellie beside me, her arm flung across my chest, her eyes watching me. The room was dark. I looked out the window. The rest of the world was dark too, except for a streetlight glowing in the distance.

"What time is it?"

"Nine, I think," Ellie said.

"What?" I sat up, the panic automatic. "My mom's going to kill—"

"Don't worry," Ellie said. "Your mom thinks you're at Lola's, still studying for a test."

My head felt foggy. It was a struggle to string words together. "But I'm not at Lola's. I'm here."

"Jess, don't make this into a thing."

"You took my phone?"

"What's the big deal? I couldn't very well text her from my phone. Then she'd know you were here." She tugged me back down so that we were both lying on our backs. "Relax. There's time."

I rolled onto my side, propping myself up on an elbow. I had so many questions, but I knew better than to ask them. "Are you feeling okay?"

"Not really." She took a deep breath and sighed.

I stared at her in the dark, her black hair fanned around her face like some kind of ironic halo. The space beneath her eyes was swollen from crying.

"Do you want me to tickle your back?" It was what my mom did for me whenever I got upset. Ellie nodded, turning away from me. I ran my fingers up and down her spine, and then I started tracing words onto her skin: "crab," "happy," "peace." Finally, when her shoulders sloped a little and I could tell she was slightly relaxed, I traced "love."

"What word was that?" She rolled over to face me. I shrugged, too nervous to speak. She took another deep breath, her eyes incredibly sad.

I touched her face lightly and said, "You really scared me. I . . . I didn't know. Are you . . ." I paused, trying to find the right question. "Does this happen a lot?" I knew that it did. The scars told me so. But I thought this might ease her into talking about it.

The look on her face told me it wasn't up for discussion. And when she changed the subject by asking me to grab her water bottle, I wasn't surprised.

Halfway there, I picked her robe up off the floor and wrapped it around me.

"No," Ellie said. "I wish you wouldn't."

I turned back to her.

"Would you take it off?" she asked.

"Ellie," I said, unsure.

"Please, Jess."

I nodded, but my hands trembled slightly as I slipped the robe onto the floor. I crossed my arms self-consciously over my belly, but she came to me and lowered them to my sides. Then she stepped back and took me in. Finally she said, "You're beautiful, Jess."

I felt so many things right then, but mostly that I wanted this moment to last forever.

She handed me the robe, and again I put it on. When she sat down, I followed—the water now forgotten—as I waited for whatever might come next. She was silent, her thoughts somewhere far off. I wanted to bring her back to me, so I said, "Ellie, are you—"

She put her finger to my lips, tears streaming down her face again. "Jess," she said, her voice hollow. "I slept with Tommy."

I was sure I hadn't heard her correctly. It seemed impossible, but then she said, her tone matter-of-fact, "It was last night. That's why I didn't text you back."

"I don't believe you. You're lying," I said, telling myself this was just another way for her to test me.

"It's true," she whispered.

I moved away from her, toward the window, and pressed my face to the cold glass. Everything inside me was shutting down, and instead of tears there was something much darker: a stark emptiness I had never felt before.

"Jess," Ellie said. "Maybe it doesn't have to be a big deal."

I flicked on the lamp beside her desk and began to dress. Ellie watched me, blinking rapidly as her eyes adjusted to the light.

"So you're just going to leave?" she asked.

"Yes." I needed to be away from her. Needed some time to think about what all of this meant. How her sleeping with Tommy but being with me were two things that might coexist.

I stopped dressing. "Can you at least tell me why?"

She shook her head. "I don't know. I had that fight with Sargeant. I didn't . . . I wasn't thinking."

CARMEN RODRIGUES

"And that makes it okay? I mean, is this what's going to happen every time you're *not* thinking?"

She stared at me blankly. "I don't know."

I started to dress again, pulling on my socks and boots, grabbing my coat.

"So that's it? We're done?" she said.

"Isn't that what you want?" She turned to stare at the wall, rapidly retreating into herself. I was tired of chasing her. I wondered what would happen if I let go. "Isn't that what you want?" I repeated.

Finally she looked at me. Her voice was flat. "Jess, don't you get it? I'll destroy you. I destroy everything."

Before, I might have gone to her, convinced her she was wrong, but the path between us was blocked now.

"So we're done?" she said.

"I guess so," I said, not sure of anything except that I wanted to hurt her as much as she hurt me.

She nodded.

At the door, I hesitated, pathetically, hoping she'd find some way to convince me to stay. But she didn't say a word. She just continued to stare at that wall.

In her mind, I was already gone.

31.

Mom saw the cuts today. I was reaching past her for a cookie. She held my hand and twisted until my forearm was raised close to her face. She looked at me, injured eyes, but didn't say a word. Typical.

Sarah
AFTER. APRIL.

Concerned Therapist enters my room at the junior psych ward. Her fake leather loafers sound less like they are shuffling and more like they are being dragged against the linoleum floor. Still, her face is perfectly composed. She has makeup on, but underneath her eyes are lines and wrinkles where she's never had them before.

She moves to the window, draws the curtain aside, and stares at who knows what. All I can see is her solemn face reflected in the dark windowpane and the hazy glow of streetlights that dot the parking lot.

I bet during her morning meditation she imagined herself heaped with blessings, a person given the power to help others break the cycles of their painful lives, but now she is faced with this, another tragedy, another person in her care that she cannot help.

With her back to me she says, "I want to help you, Sarah. I do." She turns to look at me. "Do you believe me?"

And here's the truth: I do know she wants to help me. I just don't believe that she or anyone else can.

"I guess it doesn't make a difference, does it?" Concerned Therapist offers me a weary smile. "Nothing I say or do is going to make a bit of difference to you. Is it, Sarah?"

I look at the floor and do what I always do—wait her out.

She also waits. Then she says, "Fine. Let's just get through the paperwork." Her tone has changed from concern to disinterest. The shift unsettles me. Before, when my parents came to visit, they were frantic. I expected that. When Jessie came, she was silently hysterical, and I expected that too. When Jake visited—angry and confused, and for the most part saying nothing as he held my hand—I hadn't expected that, but I was glad he came. Now, this calmness from her, this sudden distance, is something I understand but don't expect. I guess I expected conversations about my confirmed suicidal tendencies and coming to terms with my pain.

"The thing is, Sarah . . ." Disinterested Therapist flips my left hand over and stares at the bandage like she is studying it for scientific purposes. "You're entitled to take your own life. That's really your choice. I can't stop you. The only thing I can do, realistically, is delay you. I can choose to delay you for a long enough time that maybe, just maybe, you might reconsider your choices. But I can't stop you."

She releases my arm, and it falls limply onto the cotton blanket. She turns back toward the window, pulls a clipboard from the messenger bag hanging across her shoulder, and jots down a few notes. Then she stops to look at me. After a second, she sighs and returns to her scribbling.

Maybe this is reverse psychology, maybe this is just another ace up her sleeve, but I still feel scared. I don't know why it matters that Concerned Therapist cares, but it does matter.

She steps away from the window while she writes her notes, and suddenly I see my reflection. Only it can't be my reflection because it doesn't look anything like me. This is the face of someone else—some other girl with matted hair, hollow cheeks, and ghostly eyes—her lips so raw in places they're bleeding.

She shoves her clipboard in her bag and walks briskly to the door. "That's everything for today—"

"Wait." The word propels me forward, my hand stretching out toward her. "Wait!"

"What, Sarah?" Her voice is flat. "I have other patients, patients who actively participate in their own healing."

"Wait," I beg in a feeble voice. "Wait." I hate myself for sounding weak, but I don't try to stop the words from falling. "Wait." Tears slide down my cheeks. I push myself farther off the bed. "Wait."

Because the truth is: I don't know if she can help me, but I want to let her try.

"Wait. Wait. Wait. Wait," I say, and I don't stop until I feel her arms around me. She pulls me close, breaking the rules for Concerned Therapists everywhere. I hold her tightly. "Please," I say. "I need you to wait." I look up at her. Her face softens, the lines suddenly smoothed away.

She says, "I know, Sarah. I know."

At Mount Holy Oak Recovery Home, we are told to believe in a higher power. That this higher power will play a large part in our recovery. That this higher power is bigger than our worries. That this higher power has plans for us that are so big we can't comprehend them with our limited view. That the problem is that we are small and cannot see beyond our individual pain. "But God or the Universe or whatever word you would like to use for that power," the counselor tells us, "sees your lives, and we must have faith in God and the path he has chosen for us."

I came to Mount Holy Oak two weeks after my release from the hospital, and my first four nights were spent praying to God. I asked him to show me he existed. To give me a sign. Something small but significant—a shooting star, a perfectly white pigeon, a freaking rainbow on a foggy morning—but the sign never came. If God exists, it's pretty obvious he can't hear me or he's choosing to ignore me.

I'm thinking about God and divine intervention and all of that when the garden pathway leads me to Jake. He smiles when he sees me, and I smile back. It's a simple exchange—just not for us. A lot has happened in the last five months. The truth is, a lot has happened in the last five years. Still, Jake smiles at me, and for that moment I am relieved. And I wonder if this is God, if God can be found in Jake's smile.

"I'm sorry I'm late." He lays his hand on my arm. This is a significant gesture for him. Until now, he's never touched me in public. There were moments—stolen moments in Jake's pool or the basement of my house—but none of them ever strung together to make us whole. "Are you okay?" His voice is low but durable.

"Yeah, just waiting for you." We move aside to let another group pass. My stomach flips. I know this visit will be hard. I know that I'll have to tell Jake about what Jess showed me—Ellie's box with its tiny slips of paper. But I don't want to talk about the secrets. I don't even want to know them. I don't want to carry the weight of what Ellie's first stepfather did to her. Or what she did to herself.

"You want to go inside?" Jake points toward the greenhouse

in the center of the garden. "It's cold out here. I think it's going to snow." He glances at my light jacket. I wonder if he's thinking about the night in the basement. He grabs my hands, rubs them warm with the soft wool of his gray gloves. "Is that okay?"

We walk to the greenhouse in silence. Inside, Jake points to a bench tucked away beneath the barren arms of a wispy tree. We sit beside each other, our thighs touching. Jake reaches into his pocket, takes out a small folded piece of paper, and shows it to me.

"What is it?"

"A note from Tommy. He feels really bad about everything, but I know it might be too soon for you. So when you're ready for it, just ask me. Okay?" He puts it back in his pocket.

I haven't spoken to Tommy since that night by the lake, but when I was in the hospital, my mom said he called to check on me. That's the complexity of Tommy. When he knows you've been pushed too far, he stops pushing entirely.

Jake scratches his nose with his gloved hand, and then rolls his head to look directly at me. The spaces beneath his eyes are puffy, bluish bags that make him seem like he's been beaten up a lot these last few months.

"Jake?" I show him my hands. "I can't stop them from shaking."

Again he takes my hands in his. "Tell me what's going on."

"I don't know." I want to ask him for a time capsule, something that can be buried in the dirt and won't decompose—a safe place to put all of this, so we can be free. "Jake, I know about Ellie, about what happened to her."

He nods his head, and his half smile pulls down at the ends until his lips are now a thin, straight line.

"This whole time I've been going over that night. My mind just kept going over it. You know, just going in circles, and I felt this guilt. This horrible guilt, like if I had just, I don't know, been a better friend or a better person, I could have prevented it. But . . . now . . . Why didn't she tell me? Why didn't you tell me?"

My tears are big. Sloppy. My tears are the heaviness I've held inside for the last five months. I can't make the words come out anymore, but with Jake I don't need to. He holds me, and only when I tell him I'm okay again does he let go. He leans back against the bench, but continues to warm my hands between his gloved palms. He's quiet for a while, but finally he says, "I've never told anyone. Ellie and I—even we barely talked about it after it happened, after Mom got rid of him."

I feel a slight tremor in his hands. And I notice that there is a tear in his glove, and I remember that tear in his T-shirt at my twelfth birthday party. I remember Jake with his moody pout and cigarettes. Ellie with her vacant eyes and sarcastic sense of humor. Tommy, who just wanted to play jokes on everyone, to get the easy laugh. I remember me and Jake and that first kiss, the feeling of his hand pressed against my back.

"I want you to tell me," I say. "I want you to tell me everything. I want you to trust me."

He looks away, toward another family moving through the greenhouse—a father and teenage daughter, her hand clinging to his arm. The way she holds on to him makes me think about my dad, how he'd move heaven and earth if I needed him. And I think about Jake and Ellie's father, how he walked out on them when they were so young. And how in the end it doesn't matter if you have a great dad or a horrible dad, because the truth is, even with the best parents we all lose our way.

"Jake?" I drift my hand across his cheek. When our eyes meet, I lean forward and press my lips to his. His eyelashes are coated with tears. "I can't do this alone anymore."

His body tenses, and then, very quietly, he whispers near my ear, "I don't know what to do. . . . I need someone to tell me what to do." He's shaking, and I try as best I can to do what he did for me earlier. I try to hold him still. He buries his head in my shoulder and wraps his arm around my waist. And when he starts to sob, I pull him so close the air between us disappears. And there is nothing more than me and Jake, and the feeling of my hand, firm and warm, on his back.

32.

You told me this house was
made of empty bottles and
crumbling corks. You told me
we'd get out one day. But
then you went away and
forgot about me. I wasn't
surprised, though. I always
knew it would be that way.
That one day you'd be like
<u>him</u> and leave me far behind.

Jake
AFTER. MAY.

On my third visit to see Sarah at Mount Holy Oak, we search for an hour to find a private spot in the garden. Someplace where we can be alone together. There we lay out a blanket, settle down. She curls up against my chest, and soon she's more than in the crook of my arm; the full length of her is on top of me. I kiss her softly and say, "You okay?"

"This doesn't bother you? All of me on top of you?"

"No, I like you like this," I say, because I want her to know that if she needs me to, I will always carry the weight of her.

I never thought it was possible to be like this with Sarah. It's hard not to wonder how long it will last. But I tell myself to just take this like I've been taking the rest of my life: one day at a time. It's an expression Sarah uses during our phone calls, and Mom uses at home. It's an expression that's at the core of what they do here at Mount Holy Oak and, I guess, in AA. As corny as the phrase might sound, the philosophy behind it carries a certain merit.

It's an unusually sunny day. For a little while Sarah and I just lie on the grass, the sun nearly lulling us to sleep. Then I stroke her back, and we get to talking about her life here. She tells me why she likes or dislikes some of the newer residents; about her therapist, whom she wants to buy a new pair of shoes for; and about some of the staff, many of whom are kind. We talk about my life: my new job at the running store; my stepfather, who, turns out, is an okay guy; and my mom, back from rehab. When we hear others approaching, Sarah says it's time to go.

"Already?"

"Yeah. But I have a surprise."

Sarah likes surprises. She gave me one the last time I was here—a small pillow she'd made from one of her old, unwashed T-shirts. "So you don't get lonely," she said. And then she lifted the pillow to my nose. It smelled just like her—sweet with a hint of sour.

"Go this way." Sarah leads me through the garden. When the main house is in view, she wraps her arms around my waist and says, "I get out of here next month, and I was thinking that, maybe, if you want, we could go to Falling Creek together." She pauses to search my face. "We could plant flowers next to the tree where Ellie's ashes were buried. You know, maybe it's time to say some real good-byes." She puts her palm to my ribs. Her breathing is heavy. I can tell it takes a lot for her to ask this. "What do you think?"

I run my hands over my hair. I shaved it down last week, wanting a fresh start. Mom said it reminded her of a disastrous crew cut I had when I was ten, and then we were quiet for a while, because that time period reminds us of Ellie. Neither of us is sure what to do with our memories of her. Right now there's barely enough space for us.

I rest my hand on Sarah's hip and say, "I . . . Can I think about it?"

She nods, and we continue walking toward the main building. Eventually, we cut through the lobby, packed with patients. Some wear expressions like Sarah's, which vacillates between okay and not so okay. Others seem genuinely happy, laughing at something one of their family members said. These, I think, are the ones who will get out soon. And others sit quietly, staring at the wall or some piece of landscape just beyond the window. I hope these are brand-new patients, but I suspect that some of them have been to Mount Holy Oak before.

We stop in front of the art room, and she says, "I've been spending a lot of time in here lately." She leads me to a small table. "This one's mine. I mean, I have to share it with a few others, but, you know, it's still kind of mine." She pulls out the chair, and I sit. She reaches into a bin below the table and pulls out a scrapbook. "I was working on this right before you came."

Inside are photos of her and Ellie. Them at fourteen, their legs too skinny to properly fill in a pair of jeans. At sixteen, experimental streaks of red lightening Sarah's brown hair, and Ellie, looking bored, standing behind her, smoking a cigarette.

"These are from the box I sent you?" I ask, and she nods.

A few pages later I find one of me and Ellie, taken the day before I left. Ellie's cringing because I'm drunk and holding her too tight. I'm telling her the story of when she was seven and I was eight and I jumped out at her from behind a basement wall, scaring her so bad she peed her pants.

On the opposite page is Ellie's reaction. She's laughing so hard her eyes are watering. She was about to wipe away her tears when the photograph was snapped, permanently suspending her somewhere in between.

"It's not done yet," Sarah says. "But it's . . . I don't know. It helps. Somehow."

A woman's voice calls her name. Sarah turns and waves at a

young nurse with blond hair standing in the hallway. "Oh, wait. Do you mind hanging here for a sec? I want you to meet my favorite nurse. I know it's stupid to have a favorite nurse. But I told her all about you. So . . ." She walks toward the nurse. I watch them chat for a few seconds, and then I turn back to the album. I stare at Ellie's face, at her blue eyes that are the same as mine. I place my hand on the photograph and feel that familiar tear of heartbreak. I say her name aloud. I say, "Ellie." And then, because I want to remember how the word sounds coming from my mouth, I say it again. "Ellie."

And inside, I say, *I miss you, Ellie.*

I think about you every day.

I'm sorry I didn't get home in time.

I hope you'll forgive me.

And I ask her if Sarah is right, if it *is* time to say good-bye. But I don't get an answer. All I hear is the sound of Sarah, her laughter stretched out behind me. And I think that maybe it isn't time, not yet. Not for me. But I can see that one day it will be.

33.

You want me to have words.
But I have cigarettes. I have
gin. Can't you tell how I feel
by the way I touch you?

Jessie
AFTER. APRIL.

The Monday after we take Sarah to Mount Holy Oak, Mom forces me to go back to school. I'm pretty miserable by first period. That's because everyone is talking about me—even Lola, who has changed the location of her locker so it's no longer next to mine.

Maybe Mrs. Medina senses my dread. Because as soon as we settle down, she writes an essay prompt on the board: *What was the one moment that changed your life forever?*

That means today will be a silent day. Thank God.

I pull out pen and paper from my bag and set it on my desk. Then I stare at the board, thinking of the last year and all the moments that have changed me: Ellie kissing me, the stolen sketch pad, standing up to Lola, losing Ellie and then finding her box, and Sarah . . .

But even with these larger-than-life moments before me, I start writing about something safer—our move to Smith.

"This assignment totally bites ass," Lola whispers loudly behind me. A few girls snicker. I glance back and see her pass a note to Bianca. She laughs, adds something to the note, and tosses it to Melissa, who reads the note, makes a face, adds something else to it, and passes it up to Kelly. Mrs. Medina starts discussing the parameters of our essay, and I turn my attention back to the front of the classroom.

"You've got until the bell rings to complete this assignment, so that's exactly forty-five minutes. It should be roughly four pages."

"Can we skip lines?" Bobby yells from the back of the room.

Mrs. Medina gives him a tolerant look. "No, Bobby, and no cursive or excessively large letters. I want each essay to be written in your neatest print. If I can't read it, you fail. Period."

There are groans throughout the room. I notice the note is making its way toward me. Lola giggles, and I turn to look at her. She shrugs and rolls her eyes. Then she begins to write her essay.

Now the note is at my right. Clara reads it, but she doesn't laugh. She puts it in her notebook and returns to her work.

Lola whispers, "Hey, Clara, pass that on." But Clara ignores her. "*Psst*, Clara, what's your deal? Pass it on." Clara's pen freezes, but her eyes stay on her paper. "Hey, just pass the freaking note already."

Clara gives Lola a dirty look. Then she glances at me, her eyes full of sympathy. I decide to go back to my essay, but I can no longer focus. I want to know what that note says. I want to know if it's about me. Finally, I set my pen down and whisper, "It's okay, Clara. Let me see."

Clara shakes her head, crumples the note into the ball of her right hand. She opens her mouth to speak, but Lola interrupts her. "Let her see it, Clara."

Several people behind us laugh. Mrs. Medina puts aside a paper she's grading and surveys the class. "If I continue to hear this nonsense, I will cut your time."

There are more groans and the sounds of papers being shuffled as the class get back to work. Mrs. Medina returns to her grading. Clara smiles at me stiffly and whispers, "Jessie, it's so not important."

"If it's not important," Lola hisses, "then pass it."

Clara's face turns bright red, and in her outside voice she says, "You're a bitch, Lola."

From the back of the classroom, Bobby yells, "T-and-A fight!" This is followed by hoots and hollers from several guys.

Mrs. Medina snaps her grade book shut and stands up. "Class—"

"What? What did you say?" Lola asks Clara. Her voice cracks at the end.

Bobby yells, "She called you a bitch!" And this makes most of the class laugh.

The lights flick off and on. "I said"—Mrs. Medina's voice is filled with authority—"settle down." The class is immediately silent. Mrs. Medina stares at Clara, a perplexed expression on her face. She's probably trying to understand how one of her favorite students—this bubbly, confident class president who geeks, freaks, goths, and jocks all find legitimately nice—had an outburst in her class.

"I've had enough already!" Mrs. Medina shouts, even though the room is already silent. "Bobby, language like that will get you sent to the principal's office. And you know how your father is when I call home!" She walks toward Clara's desk, her palm out. Clara hands her the note. She reads it silently, her face solemn. She looks from me to Lola, takes a huge breath, and says, "Lola, I'll see you after class."

"Mrs. Medina, that's not mine—"

"Stop," Mrs. Medina snaps. "Just stop. We'll discuss this after class when we can call your parents."

"What?" Lola's eyes are watery, and the cockiness slips from her face. "But what about Clara? Are you going to call her parents?"

Mrs. Medina shakes her head. "I suggest you worry about the consequences of your own actions and leave Clara to me."

A few kids gasp. Mrs. Medina is never this tough. Need a bathroom pass? No problem. Have to run to your locker? No problem. An extension on your homework assignment? Sure. Mrs. Medina always gives the benefit of the doubt.

"Class!" Mrs. Medina's voice moves our attention from Lola to her. "You have exactly thirty-five minutes to complete your essay. I suggest you start now."

The class protests. Mrs. Medina raises her hand, and again there is silence. "If you have an issue with the grade you receive on this essay, I suggest you find the time to take it up with Lola *after class*."

There is another collective groan. Several people from the upper rows turn to glare at Lola.

Everyone can hear Lola crying. I don't turn around, but I imagine her face looks the same as it did the afternoon we spied on Tommy.

I feel strange. I look at Clara. She's busy working on her essay. I glance back at Lola. Her head is on her desk, her legs curled up onto her seat, like she's trying to disappear.

I take out a clean sheet of paper and start writing—not about my move to Ohio, but about my first kiss with Ellie. My hand moves swiftly across the page, the first of many secrets escaping.

After class, I head for the school's double doors. I'm expecting security to pounce on me or an alarm to sound, but there is nothing. Just concrete steps, the flagpole, a whole lot of brown grass, and me, breathing in the icy air.

It's supposed to snow today. A spring snowstorm that doesn't seem so freakish now that it's happened several times in the last few years. *The world is changing. Nothing fits where it's supposed to. Even the snow is confused,* Mom said yesterday. We were sitting on the couch, everyone except Sarah, and I could tell from the way she kept looking around, she missed her. I missed her too.

The night before Sarah left for Mount Holy Oak, Mom called Sarah and me into the kitchen and said, "Sometimes you want to save someone, but you can't. Some people—like Ellie— want to stay lost, and if someone wants to stay lost, there's nothing you can do to help them. You just pray that one day they'll find their way." She grabbed our hands and pulled them close to her heart. "But you never blame yourself for what anyone else does, the choices they make." She looked at me, her eyes wet.

"There's been too much bad stuff. And I couldn't take losing either of you, okay?"

Afterward, I decided it was time to show Ellie's box to Sarah.

"What is it?" she asked when I set it between us on my bed.

"It belonged to Ellie."

"Is it about you?" She looked away, cleared her throat, and then turned back to me, her brown eyes serious. "Is it about you and Ellie? You know . . . being together."

I stared at her, slightly stunned.

"I found this . . ." She stood and went to her closet. She took out a slightly larger box and set it on the bed beside the shoe box. She slid off the lid and reached inside, past dozens of photos of Ellie, and pulled out a notebook. From the pages of the notebook she removed a single Polaroid of me sleeping peacefully on Ellie's freckled shoulder. Ellie must have taken it the night of our last fight.

I didn't know what to say. And maybe I didn't need to; maybe the tears streaming down my face said it all.

Sarah pulled me close and held me for a while. When I moved away, she nodded toward the shoe box. "What's in it?"

"I guess," I said, my voice rough, "I guess it's also about all of us—you, me, Jake, Tommy, Ellie's mom. It's what Ellie felt about all of us."

I read the hesitancy in her face. She said, "I can't . . . Not yet."

"When you're ready . . . ," I said, and then I set the box on the top shelf of my closet, and asked her if she would tell me about Ellie's final hours.

And so she began to talk about that night, how Ellie didn't seem like herself, how she seemed incredibly sad but also determined to pretend she was happy. "If I'd known everything, I'd have never let her near those pills. But I didn't know, you know? I just . . ." Her voice faded. She was crying, but she continued on, and near the end she told me about the hot-pink fishnet stockings Ellie had worn that night.

The stockings were my only gift to Ellie, and I remembered how surprised she'd been when I'd handed her the small box with its purple ribbon, and how she'd put them on immediately and in a matter of minutes picked them apart, exposing both her knees.

And the crazy thing is, out of everything Sarah told me, Ellie dying in something as outrageous as those stockings made the most sense. I don't know why, but it did.

"Do you think," Sarah said, looking out the window toward Ellie's house, "that she did it . . ." She stalled, but I knew that she wanted to ask the questions I had been asking since Ellie died. Did she have a plan to end it that night? Or was it just a hasty decision made in a moment of extreme sadness and pain? Or maybe it was as my mom had said that morning—an accident?

I stared out the window too, thinking about all the times I had seen Ellie walking in and out of her house. It was hard to believe I'd never see her again. That she'd never tell me if she ever really loved me. "I guess we'll never know," I finally said.

I continue to think about Ellie now, as I walk these long blocks from school. And I find myself somewhere I never intended—at Falling Creek, standing in front of the tree that bears her name. I drop my bag and kneel at its base, running my fingers over the plaque's deeply cut letters. I lay my head against the bark, pressing my cheek to its fractured skin. I tell myself that somewhere above, Ellie watches. I tell myself she is no longer alone.

An hour later, snow begins to fall, coating the tree's stark branches, resting in clumps along the joints. My face is cold, but I'm not worn down by the chill. I am something else entirely.

I stand, pulling my jacket tightly across my shoulders, lifting the hood over my head. I hug my bag to my chest. I blink rapidly and look out at the world just beyond: the brown, patchy grass. A rusted car. The world is still shaky, but not for long. By nightfall the streets will be blanketed in crisp white snow, and everything will look clean again. Everything will feel possible again.

I take one step forward and then another. And soon, I am home.

34.

I like to remember trips to
Cedar Point. The summer wind
warm on our backs. Candied
apples and neon-green bracelets
glowing at night. And Jake on
Dad's shoulders, too tired to
walk, and Mom holding my hand.

Author's Note

Dear Reader,

Like Ellie, there have been times when I've felt incredibly alone. Over the years, I've learned that the key to surviving the darkest days is to ask for help. So if you or someone you know struggles with depression or suicidal thoughts, I urge you to reach out to a trustworthy friend, family member, or adult who will listen and offer support. If someone is not readily available, then explore outside resources, such as the ones listed on the next page. Each is accessible 24–7 and is staffed by caring individuals.

Life is hard, but it's also crazy-beautiful. Fight for your best life. You deserve it.

With love,
Carmen

Resources

ONLINE

TeenCentral.net

This safe website allows you to post your questions, problems, or thoughts anonymously and receive an answer within a twenty-four-hour period. You can also read other teens' stories and respond to them with your own thoughts and counseling—again, this is anonymous. This is a great site to find help, hope, and answers from counselors and even other teens while maintaining your anonymity. Log on and work it out!

OFFLINE

Try any of these help lines, which offer live, around-the-clock support.

National Youth Crisis Hotline: 1-800-448-4663

Childhelp: 1-800-422-4453

National Suicide Prevention Lifeline: 1-800-273-TALK